Chronicles of Ériu Series.

Volume 1 – The Demise of Affreidg.
Volume 2 – Cessair's Hegira.
Volume 3 – The Land of Plenty.
Volume 4 – The Fomorians.
Volume 5 – The Bronze Age.
Volume 6 – Tír na nÓg (Not published yet.)
Volume 7 – Partholon. (Not published yet.)

ISBN: 978-0-9956214-3-5

Published by Waring Estate Publication.
Email   publication@waringestate.com.
         Info@chroniclesoferiu.co.uk

Printed: Waring Estate Publications.

THE CHRONICLES OF ÉRIU.

VOLUME 3.

The Land of Plenty.

BY

MICHAEL H ST.C HARNETT

ILLUSTRATED BY KASEY LEITCH

The Chronicles of Ériu – The Land of Plenty

This book is dedicated to

The Brehons and Bards of ancient Ireland who, for many millennia, dedicated their lives to the memory of the Irish experience so that we may understand it today.

It is my great wish that their dedication is now recognised and appreciated as their interpretation of our shared history, rather than as just a fanciful rendering of myths and legends.

Glossary

Affreidg – Cessair's birth land, now flooded by the Black Sea.

Ancients – Those spirits, gods, and people of prehistory.

Angus – leader of the axe-making tribe on Rathlin Island.

Antonio – Santorinian sea trader

Api – Mother Nature

Balor – Leader of the Formorians

Banba – Cessair's 'right hand' woman and later a tribe leader.

Bards – Irish chroniclers and storytellers.

Bith – Cessair's father.

Bóinne – Boyne River settlement area of great holy importance.

Brehons – The interpreters and administrators of the law.

Bridget – A powerful female druid (a spiritual leader)

Broadhaven – Ériu's third settlement.

Cailtach – Female Druid High Priestess, a spiritual leader.

Capa – Iberian doctor and wright (good at making things.)

Cessair – The leader of the first tribes in Ériu.

Curragh – A small boat made of branches and animal hides.

Dûn na m-Barc – The fortress of the boats.

Druid – Spiritual leaders

Ériu – The 'Land of Plenty' now called Ireland.

Fintan – Inventor and Cessair's husband

FirBolg – Literally 'The Bag Men' – men who moved soil & rock.

FirGaileoin – Men who 'speared' (dug) the ground.

Fomorians – Those who came from under the sea.

Giza – Egyptian Holy centre and future site of the Pyramids

Hippolyte – Amazonian warrior princess.

Kallisti – Sardinian trader and former explorer.

Ladra – Cessair's childhood friend, Sea captain & shipbuilder.

Laigni – From Iberia, collected 'exotics' in Ériu to sell in Iberia.

Ley Lines – Spirit communication lines.

Li – The river Bann

Luasad - Iberian (now Spain) fisherman

Manandan – Ériu's God of the sea

Merkhet - Instrument of knowing or pendulum

Meroe – Cessair's home in Egypt.

Partholon – Scythian tribe leader and businessman

Saball – Egypt's Pharaoh, Cessair's foster father.

Santorini – Mediterranean island proficient in making copper items.

Saqqara – Early Egyptian Holy centre

Scotia – Cessair's Goddaughter and Saball's granddaughter.

Sherden – Sardinian Sea traders.

Sí an Bhrú – Newgrange, the Boyne holy settlement.

Tabiti – Scythian main god.

Waterford – Ériu's first settlement and primary town.

Wexford – Ladra's coastal port town.

1
Is it there that they came to the harbour,
The woman crowd, at Dun na mBarc.
In the nook of Cessair, in the lands of Carn,
On the fifteenth, on Saturday.

The Taking of Ireland. (Poem XXVIII)

2 *They reached great Ireland*
Far from the Pillars of Hercules;
They took kingship over every hill-fort
That was in Ireland before them.
3 *As a wright and a leech are those celebrated,*
And a ruthless fisherman:

...

6 *When they reached Ireland,*
The three champions without religion,
Noble Ireland was explored by them
From the Li-estuary to Spain

...

9 *Those are the details of the three,*
The first who invaded Ireland with valour.
They left Ireland without progeny,
Luasad, Laigni, and Capa.

The Taking of Ireland. (Poem XXII)

Contents of Volume Three.

New Start, New Rules, New Spirits, and a New Nation.

New Start, New Rules, New Spirits, and a New Nation.

"Taste this!" said Bith as he handed Cessair a small hazel nut. Cessair just popped it into her mouth and was about to bite when her father shouted, ***"Wait!*** *Take the shell off first."*

Cessair watched as Bith set the small nut on a rock and gently hit it with a small stone. He handed the small inner nut saying,

"This is the bit to eat. The trees around here are full of them. If we gather them up, then we will have good food for the coming winter."

As Cessair ate the tasty nut and looked at the large bag of them that her father had gathered, in just a few minutes, she thought, *"Ériu is the land of plenty, and Api has given us another great feast just waiting to be gathered up."*

1

The river island of Dûn na m-Barc gave Cessair and her tribes a safe toehold for their taking of Ériu. Kallisti's directions and advice had proved invaluable to Cessair and her people, but they fell well short in describing Ériu's true beauty and fecundity. Cessair had named the country well.

It had been well over seven years since they were driven out of Affreidg by that evil sea god. After seven years of preparation and waiting, thousands of miles of travel and discovery, and now the future of this new nation was housed in a temporary camp close to the confluence of three rivers. In the middle of one of the rivers was a small island. It was big enough to accommodate the temporary camp, and it gave them protection from any possible outsider attack, animal or human. The island reminded her of Meroe, her home in Egypt, and she was tempted to name it after that place; however, here, the ships were all moored around this island, so Cessair named it: 'Dûn na m-Barc.'

There were almost a thousand people when all of the boats were discharged. There were plenty of people to defend themselves from possible attack but far too many for long-term accommodation that depended on a sustainable, hunting and scavenging food supply. Cessair knew things had to change, and they had to change quickly. They had been brought up as farmers, but for the next year or so, they would have to become hunter-gatherers until their crops had time to establish and grow.

The first few days, many were busy. Some were gathering fruits and nuts, while others were hunting the forests and fishing the rivers for food. Yet others were creating fences and paddocks to pen their sheep, cattle, and other stock that they had brought with them.

Cessair had sent exploratory expeditions, in small boats, up the three rivers, into the heartland of Ériu. All around them were dense forests of ancient and massive trees. None of them had ever seen trees that were so large, and no one knew that so many different types of trees existed together and that all could have so much wildlife.

2

New Start, New Rules, New Spirits, and a New Nation.

Ladra left with two ships to circle Ériu. He sent two ships together in case one ran into difficulties. They were to search out the other rivers that could support new settlements by giving shelter, access, farming land and a ready food supply. Bridget and some other druids were also on board. It was their responsibility to rate any potential settlement area for its spiritual suitability and harmony with Api. It was essential for any tribe to be able to live in sympathy and alongside, and not harm, the spirits that lived all around in the earth, water, plants, and trees.

There were, now living in Ériu, four shiploads of people who had less physical work to do, but their responsibilities soon became the most important of all. After a few days, Cessair called them all together and addressed them as two groups. The first group were the two shiploads of people tasked with defining the laws.

"Before we left Troy, I separated you into a shipload of women and one of the men. You were asked to create laws under which all of the citizens of Ériu would follow and obey. I separated you because I wanted the new rules to respect both sexes without undue influence from either side. You were given only one rule as your starting point: the single word 'Respect.' Both groups independently created remarkably similar rules, which gives me great confidence that they will work."

Cessair now changed her tone, just as she had learned from Ardfear and Saball, from one of explanation to one of proclamation.

"From now on, you will all be 'The Brehons.' You will be the people who interpret and uphold the law. You will be associated with your original tribe and also be part of a new wider community of Brehons throughout Ériu. The Brehon Laws that you have created have been based on respect; they will be the same for all tribes in Ériu. It will be your job, as individual tribe council members, to

ensure that the laws are in line with those of the other tribes throughout Érui. This will now become your profession forever; your children should follow the same profession for their lives as well as their offspring.

Many of you came as representatives of tribes that are now left back in Troy; they wish to follow us here soon. It will be your job to return to them and to teach each of your tribes the new rules. These laws are now mandatory for all citizens of Érui. If they cannot accept these rules that will define our way of life in Érui, then your tribe should not adventure across the Endless Sea to come here!"

There was great discussion amongst the newly appointed Brehons, but there was overwhelming support for Cessair's proclamation. Now Cessair addressed the second group,

"In Troy, I gave you no such task, but I now also give you a new profession. From now on, you will be known as 'Bards;' you will be the keepers and chroniclers of our history. As with the Brehons, you will represent your profession in tribal council meetings and have equal influence as them. It will be your duty to ensure that our tribes will learn from mistakes made in the past by any of our tribes and to advocate against repeating those mistakes while council meetings are discussing strategy. You will also be responsible for maintaining our history alive by educating our young and our visitors.

For those of you whose tribes are not yet here, it will be your duty to tell them of Érui before they come."

The first week saw three new tribe members born. There were grand celebrations at this real show of faith in the future. Api must be happy with the tribe to allow such blessings. The three children

4

were named *Suir*, Barrow and Nore, and in honour of these first births in Ériu, Cessair named the three rivers around them after these precious gifts from Api.

Bith had spent the first few days exploring the immediate area and searching out a place for their first permanent settlement. The choice of site was to be one of the most important decisions that he had to make. The site had to support the fledgling tribe and its few domesticated animals and be able to grow his precious seeds. It needed fresh water but not flood, protection from the worst of the weather but still making the best of the sunlight. They had to be close to food sources but still offer protection from wild animals. The site chosen for the first settlement was crucial and not to be taken lightly.

*"This is **the** place I was taken to."*

Said Bith to the small party that was sitting in the little boat as they rowed up the river Suir. The river had broadened out and was much shallower. The dense woodland had thinned out on either side, and there were two large areas of lush grasses.

"When I first explored the woods around Dûn na m-Barc, I saw a giant Elk; it was much bigger than any deer I have ever seen anywhere; I never thought that they could grow so big. It had huge antlers that were much wider than my arms at full width. I approached him quietly several times, but each time he walked away. I meant him no harm, and I swear he knew it. After a while, I stopped following, and it also stopped and looked back at me. I approached it again, and again it walked off; it was as though he was leading me.

I followed this majestic animal until the woods thinned, and we entered this grassy plain by the bend in the river. He then walked back, came up close to me, and looked down, straight into my eyes, as if to say, 'You are safe here.' I turned to look around me, and when I turned back - he was gone. I heard nothing, and I could not even find his tracks. It is as though Tabiti herself had sent him."

Cessair and Banba stood in amazement at the story of such a divine creature. Even the practical Fintan was captivated by the story of the giant ethereal stag. None of his companions even thought to question Bith's recollection, but instead, all were overjoyed that such a regal animal should guide them to such a place.

"This place is perfect."

Were Banba's first words followed by,

"If I fence here, there will be plenty of grazing for our animals. We can build our houses near the river, here on this small hill. If we ever do come under attack in the future, we are close to Dûn na m-Barc, where, if necessary, we can retreat to."

Cessair looked around and then back to the river before saying,

"Water-Ford! The place where the river is shallow enough for us to cross. The name of this our first settlement will also remind our children of how we had to cross the great water of the Endless Sea to come to Ériu. This will become a great seat of learning and be at the heart of our great nation."

Hundreds of people were building round houses on the small hill the following day. They also surrounded the whole village with a fence made of woven saplings. Fintan marked out the foundations of the first roundhouse; a circle was drawn with a rope pinned to the ground at one end. The roundhouse was six paces across. He spoke to the workers around him.

"I want sixteen holes around this circle. In each hole, I want tree trunks as wide as my foot, buried and standing upright about my height. They are to be support for the roof. Interlace saplings between the trees around the circle but leave one gap open as a door. Take wet clay from the river and build up walls around the saplings. When it's dry, it will become hard and very strong. Use smaller trees for the roof; they will meet at a point above the middle of the house, just like the poles of our travelling tents. Then cover the whole roof

with reeds cut from the riverbanks so the rain will run down them and out, and not unto the house."

With so many people working, Waterford village had taken shape within days and was completed in less than a month. They became so good at building houses that at the end of the main building work, they had made one massive, long house capable of sheltering one small tribe. This was to be a grand communal hall.

The first of Cessair's tribes now had its first permanent home in over seven years. Winter would soon be arriving, and they all knew that they had much to do before the days shortened and Ériu's supply of uncollected nuts and fruits would be gone.

Cessair's scouts returned from their expeditions; they had travelled up the three rivers to explore and report back. Each scout leader was equally enthusiastic and only too keen to talk about what they had found.

"The river waters were so clear, and everywhere we went, they were full of great big fish. The river oysters were as big as my fist. We travelled upriver for days. The river became very small, but we could still use our curraghs. Where there were rocks or rapids that we could not pass, we just carried our boats over or around them."

Started one spokesman. Another continued,

"This is certainly the land of plenty. Api has excelled here! Many animals, including tasty boar, were in the great woods of fine timber. Others, such as deer, were in large areas of green grass; even the waters were full of food. Among the grasses, we found many cereals with seeds that we could harvest – not as good as Bith's seeds, but it also shows that they will grow here. We found many

places where we could set up new villages, and we could set them up very quickly with the local materials."

All of the tribes on the island, still in temporary accommodation, were keen to move on as soon as possible. The autumn equinox would occur soon, and they all wanted to be resettled before the end of the year and be in their new homes, ready for the following year's rebirth. Despite all of the excitement raised by the scouts' good news, there was one crucial voice that everyone wanted to hear. It was that of Bridget, the head druid. However, her voice would not be heard until she returned from the sea trip with Ladra. Even then, she would not speak publicly until the first Grand Council in Ériu, which was to be held on the day of the next equinox.

A few days later, Cessair saw Banba rushing up to her in great excitement. A slightly breathless Banba had exciting news, and Cessair had to hear it.

"Ladra's ships are back! The two ships were coming up the estuary towards the Suir, probably docking at Dûn na m-Barc by now. I was visiting some of our people that are making salt down by the sea when I saw two ships going past. One looked badly damaged; many people were on board bailing out water!"

Cessair immediately set off in the direction of the dock, and the quickest way to travel the short distance downriver to the fortress island was by curragh. She wanted to find out what had happened and hear what they had found out about Ériu.

Only one boat was tying up at the dock when Cessair and an even more breathless Banba arrived to find a beleaguered Ladra ready to greet them on board. Cessair's first words were.

"Where is your second boat? Banba saw it at sea, and was it damaged?"

"It is badly damaged but not lost. We ran it aground back in the tidal estuary. The tide was very high, so we left it high up on the sand. The very high tide means it will be safe and out of the water for the next few days, and we will have time to repair it before the tides are as high again. We were caught in stormy seas as we left a river three days ago. Bridget and the other druids were so excited with what they had discovered that our attention was elsewhere, and then a wave lifted the ship and crashed it down upon a rock. The broken keel let in water. We emptied the water as quickly as it came in by using a chain of people passing buckets up through the ship. Everyone worked day and night to keep the ship afloat long enough for us to return. Both crews took turns bailing out the seawater; both crews are now exhausted. Manandan did preserve us on the sea, and we do have a lot to thank him for."

Ladra looked as though he could just lie down and sleep on the deck; he had nothing more to give. Cessair sent him off to sleep. She had to wait for her answers, just a little longer, until after Ladra and the crew took a few hours of well-earned rest.

It was only a few hours before Ladra was back with Cessair, telling her the news.

"Ériu is much bigger than we thought. It took us almost all of the time just to sail around it. There are very many big rivers that lead into its heart. The south has big, long estuaries with high mountains on either side. The west has the biggest seas we have ever seen and at least one huge and promising river. The land behind also has many mountains. The north has many more long sandy beaches, and the east is much more sheltered, with more woodland and some

open grassland. We could not stop on the last part of our journey; we will have to go back soon; it looks great."

Cessair asked if they had met or seen anyone else.

"We did see a ship in the distance when we were off the west coast. But most importantly, we met the people in the north that Kallisti was talking about. They are living on a small island just north of Ériu. Here! Look at this."

Ladra handed Cessair a perfectly smooth black stone axe.

"Be careful. Its edge is very sharp. I exchanged a number of these for some of our supplies and pots. They are sharper and harder than any that I have ever seen before. These are the axes that Kallisti was telling us about. We could quickly sell these at a good profit back in Troy.

The west coast was full of those seashells with purple dye. There is a fortune worth of those shells; they are just waiting to be picked up. Ériu is full of things that we can trade."

Cessair heard about the many areas where the tribes could settle and the many practical reasons why they should. There was, however, one more person she wanted to talk to; someone crucial to the tribe's spiritual acceptance of and by, Ériu.

Cessair first met Bridget in Egypt about five years earlier. She was a member of one of the Scythian tribes that were building the monuments in Giza. Like Cessair's childhood friend Dana, Bridget studied magic and astrology all of her life. She was a powerful druid before she reached Egypt, but after training in Egyptian astrology and magic, she had become one of the best.

Bridget, Cessair and Scotia had spent many days on Cessair's island, Meroe, learning how to interpret the movements of a pendulum and its reactions to the spiritual world. Bridget was now to be found in the dense woods where the ancient spirits possessed the trees. She and the other travelling druids had rushed back to their homes as soon as they had landed so they may discuss with the rest of the druids.

Cessair had just crossed the river from Dûn na m-Barc and was about to head into the woods when she was surprised to see Bridget coming the other way, and Bridget was looking for her.

"I have so much to tell you; we need to talk now!"

Blurted out a normally calm Bridget. The two sat under a vast Elm tree on the bank of the River Suir, and then Bridget started.

"Remember how back in Meroe we used to discuss and argue with the Egyptian priests about our world and its creation. The priests said that the gods had formed our world from chaos and had left us here to enjoy it, and it was our duty to thank them for it constantly. Our Scythian ancestors, however, taught us that the gods had made our world from chaos, but most importantly, they are still fashioning it. We were taught that our role is to help the gods fashion the world around us and to respect and enjoy their ancient labours and our combined works.

Cessair knew all this and could not see why Bridget was so excited, but she listened quietly until she heard Bridget's words.

*"I can now show that we Scythians **were** right!"*

Now Cessair thought, *"This will be interesting; no one can prove the presence of a god. What is Bridget going to say next?"*

"Come with me to Waterford, where I will show you that the spirits of the gods are all around us and that they will help us if we ask them."

New Start, New Rules, New Spirits, and a New Nation.

Bridget's excited words reminded her of her friend Dana when, as children, they found something new and important. Bridget was already rushing ahead, leaving Cessair behind. Bridget was on her mission to reveal a natural and spiritual wonder, and no dawdling chieftain was going to slow her down.

Cessair caught up with her when she stopped at a hazel tree. Cessair knew this tree because it was like the one that had the tasty nuts that her father had first given her. As Cessair reached the tree, Bridget spoke again.

"The spirits are everywhere, and there is one in this tree now, and it will help us. Like this tree, there is one essential we all need every day. It is fresh, pure water; this spirit will help us find it in our new town."

Before Cessair could even answer, Bridget had taken a small, forked branch from the hazel tree and was again rushing towards the village. Cessair was starting to worry about her friend, so she picked up her own pace just to catch up with her.

When Cessair managed to reach Bridget, they were already in the new village. Bridget held the forked hazel branch by the two finer ends, one end in each hand. Her arms were out in front of her, and the branch was horizontal, with the thicker part pointing straight forward. She was walking around the village in meditative silence. Her behaviour looked strange, so several people joined Cessair as she followed Bridget. No one spoke out loud, but there soon was a buzz of expectation. Bridget slowly walked up and down and around until, just as she was walking up a slope, the branch rapidly moved upwards. Everyone gasped and watched in amazement. Bridget marked the spot and headed off again; the small branch was again horizontal. A few minutes later, the branch again jumped, only this time more violently. Bridget again marked the spot before speaking to Cessair.

"The spirit of the tree has spoken to me, and its message is loud and clear. There is water under these two places that I have marked."

Cessair looked doubtful, and Bridget could see it in her eyes. Bridget spoke again.

New Start, New Rules, New Spirits, and a New Nation.

"I know from the pendulums in Meroe that you, too, know how to commune with the spirits. Here, hold this hazel branch like this, and walk around, the way I was. Do not try to overthink anything but imagine that you are looking for water."

Cessair took the branch to humour Bridget, but she did try to think that she was looking for water. She walked around for several minutes with, by now, a large crowd following her. Her concentration on the water was lost as she started to think.

"I am starting to make a fool of myself. I must........"

Her thoughts were cut short when the hazel branch tip positively leapt straight up.

"I did not do that!"

Yelped Cessair; she was so shocked that she dropped the branch.

"Yes, you did; you did with the help of the living spirit of the wood."

Said Bridget as she marked the spot on the ground before speaking to the assembled crowd.

"Please dig these three places."

Cessair was taken aback by what had just happened. She just stood there, silently thinking.

"I did not move that stick. I was playing along with Bridget and was just about to stop when the branch jumped. What just happened?"

Cessair just felt a gentle tug as Bridget took her into a nearby hut to sit down and compose her thoughts. She had never before experienced her body taking direction from anyone but her conscious mind.

A few minutes later, a tribesman came rushing in just as Cessair was regaining her composure. He was shouting.

"Come look"

She and Bridget followed the tribesman to the place where the stick jumped in her hand. There in front of her was a freshly dug hole, and bubbling up from the bottom was clear water. Someone took a mug of it and handed it to Cessair as the first to taste it. She put it to her lips and then spoke.

"This is the purest water I have ever tasted."

She paused to think for a moment and then continued,

"Why wouldn't it be; it was given to us by the gods. The spirits are with us and all around us."

She then made a little silent prayer to Tabiti.

"Thank you. I know that your spirits are with us and that you will keep us safe. I now know that you also sent that Ancient in Elk form to my father to guide us – thank you."

Cessair's first Grand Council in Ériu.

There were very few tribes in Ériu, so necessarily there should have been very few members attending the first Grand Council. There were, however, representatives from fifty tribes, many of those tribes were still back in Troy. Cessair declared that all of the Druids, Bards and Brehons in Ériu were required to attend.

The Grand Council, back in the days of Affreidg, was always a time of celebration and party. Even the last Grand Council before their ancient homeland was flooded started as one. This time, however, there was plenty to celebrate, and there were no 'black clouds' to dampen anyone's spirits. They had safely made it to Ériu. They had built their first town, gathered stores for the winter and above all, their gods were helping them. Many people were lighting fires and preparing a sumptuous feast while the delegates were all crammed into the longhouse.

Cessair rose to speak and started.

"I welcome you all to the first Grand Council gathering in Ériu."

But before she spoke another word, someone in the room shouted.

"Cessair is our great leader – hurrah!"

The whole room erupted in cheers and applause. Next to her, Fintan, Banba, Ladra, Bridget and even Bith were all cheering as loudly and enthusiastically as everyone else. Over seven years of escaping, waiting, preparing, and then travelling were over, and the spirits of everyone ran high. It was several minutes before Cessair could speak, and secretly she was glad of the time so that she could control the upwelling of emotions and wipe away the tears that were starting to well in the sides of her eyes.

"Everyone of us did this together with the help and guidance of Tabiti."

Another great cheer but this time, Cessair waited only a few moments and then she spoke on.

"We have achieved so much together, but we still have many things to achieve before the end of the year. We have built one fine village ...."

Another great cheer. Cessair paused briefly and then continued.

"Next week, we will start two more. One is about half a day's travel upriver, and the other, also less than a day away, but this time it will be situated up the coast. Fintan will take some people upriver to where there is another great site and lots of local food still available to gather. Ladra will take another group up the coast.

The two hundred representatives from the tribes left back in Troy will be split between the two new sites and will help to build the new villages quickly. Waterford will remain our centre and will support new tribes when they arrive, and it will offer them a chance to recover before they establish new settlements elsewhere in Ériu."

There was surprise at the news, but all those without homes in Waterford were glad at the prospect of living in proper homes for the main winter. The nomadic tents they were living in, in Dûn na m-Barc, were small, cold and could be wet; the prospect of their own roundhouse seemed like a perfect dream. Cessair waited for a few seconds before continuing.

"During the winter, we can build implements and prepare the land, ready for our seeds in spring. Ladra will send most of our ships back to Troy early next year and return with more of our tribes. There are many things that we can trade from Ériu. Ladra will bring

samples of them with him to show Antonio, Partholon and the other Mediterranean traders."

Cessair went on with several administrative announcements before asking Bridget to speak for the Druids and their findings in Ériu. Most people were scared of Bridget, and some even secretly thought that she was a little crazy. They could not understand what she did or how she did it, which frightened them; nevertheless, everyone stood in awe of her abilities. Bridget slowly stood, and there was immediate total silence. Then she spoke.

"In Egypt, we saw the power of the spirits, especially those in the land. We could talk with them by using our Merkhets, our instruments of knowing; they are also called pendulums. This stone at the bottom came from an island in the Red Sea. It is called Topaz and is only found on that island."

Bridget took her Merkhet from around her neck, unhooked one end and held the thread by the clasp. The other end of the thread was tied to a small, carved stone that swung below. At first, the pendulum swung to and fro, but the pattern soon changed to a circular motion.

"The spirits, through me, control the motions of this merkhet. The way that the pendulum moves is how they talk through me. Up until now, the movements were the strongest in Giza, and that is the reason why we chose that area to build great monuments in that part of Egypt."

Bridget looked around the room with a great grin on her face, and then she continued.

"I have never heard the spirits so clearly as I do here in Ériu, and never before have they talked to us druids so loudly. They are pleased that we are here and want us to help them to fashion Ériu in the future."

She waited for the news to sink in, and for the council members to understand what she had just said. A few seconds later, the news that the spirits were welcoming them and wanted their human help to shape Ériu brought a joyous roar of approval. Cessair thought it the right time for the Grand Council to end and the celebratory party to begin.

Cessair and Fintan walked around the village, looking and tasting all the great foods being prepared. This was not just a party around the harvest equinox, it was a celebration of everything good in their new world. It was a time to relax, take stock of their lives and a time for them to live and enjoy life in harmony with Api.

There was music and singing; some people were dancing, and the children played. There were fires with wild boar on spits above them; some had a smaller game like the Great Hare or wild geese. Other areas had fish such as salmon and oysters from the rivers and mackerel and shellfish from the sea. There were tables with nuts like hazel and acorns and fruits such as raspberries and blackberries, and even parts of the wild water lilies were being cooked. Even the three wells, found with the help of the hazel spirit, had been finished and protected by large stones, and they were now supplying clean, fresh water. Cessair turned to Fintan and spoke.

"Api has everything we need, and she is so generous to us, and yet most of the people of our world want more and to control it; they will even fight to assert their power over it. We cannot let that happen in Ériu. We have to share this our new home with the spirits that are helping us so that our children can also love and preserve Ériu for our future."

*"**Our** children?"*

Asked Fintan meaningfully.

Cessair's first Grand Council in Ériu.

Cessair became silent, and her mood mellowed.

Fintan was wise enough to give her time for her thoughts. With the responsibilities of being a leader at such an early age, her duties in Egypt and her foster child taking such a vital part of her life, she never really thought much about her marriage and her own children.

Cessair was a healthy young woman, and she was missing Scotia. Even though Scotia was not her natural child, she had grown to love her with all her heart; Cessair also knew that she wanted children of her own. Fintan was incredibly special to her, and he had always remained close to her throughout their time in Egypt. He was her best friend and aide. Then she remembered the spark that was lit all those years ago in her grandfather's house in Affreidg. She realised that it had never really gone away, and now she knew that

Fintan would make a great companion and father. He was unlike Ladra, who had one wife after another, none lasting more than a year or two; his next great adventure was always over the horizon. Fintan was always there; he was always there for her. When they left Giza for the last time, she remembered how safe she felt while weeping onto his chest while his strong arms cocooned her in a warm, comforting hug.

She took Fintan's hand and held it firmly. She had held his hand many times – but never quite like this. She turned and looked straight into his eyes and said with a calm understatement.

"Yes! Our children!"

The party in Waterford went on for most of that night. No one had to be up early the following morning.

Fintan's new village was not far up the river Barrow. The place chosen was close to where the river was divided into two smaller rivers. The river was large enough to allow one of the ships to be used as a ferry, carrying many people or goods simultaneously. The use of the big ship allowed Fintan's village to be established very quickly and in time to gather the last of the local harvest to sustain them through the winter.

It took time and effort to row and pull the big ship upriver unless the wind helped by blowing from directly behind them. However, returning downriver, along with the current, took almost no effort and the journey only took about an hour.

Ladra's new village also made use of big ships. He had chosen the next big estuary just up the coast. The coastline had many of those seashells containing the valuable dye. There was also plenty of safe and protected anchorage where the big ships could safely wait out the winter storms. While Waterford was situated on a constantly flowing freshwater river, Wexford had all of the advantages of being on the seacoast with only the predictable tide to worry about, and it was, therefore, a better place for seafarers.

"It is hard to believe that it has only been six weeks since the Grand Council, and now it is the Day of the Dead."

Said Fintan as he and Cessair were walking alone towards the ceremony to celebrate the end of the year.

"Yes, so much has happened, and with all of my travelling between the three towns, we have hardly even seen each other. Tomorrow I will announce our marriage agreement at the festival at the start of the New Year. Many other couples are announcing their connection tomorrow; I know as I had to approve them."

"Did you approve ours?"

Asked Fintan as he squeezed her hand and offered a cheesy grin.

"I will think about it!"

Replied Cessair with an equally big grin.

The Day of the Dead had always been an important calendar marker for any Scythian tribe. It was celebrated halfway between the Autumn Equinox and the Winter Solstice. Now for Cessair and her tribe, this day was a particularly important one. Everyone had travelled to Waterford for this key event, and many were back in their nomad tents for the days of ceremonies.

Bridget, the leader of the Druids, opened the ceremony with the words.

"We must all thank Tabiti for safely bringing us through another year and for providing us with such a wonderful harvest. We must now ask her to accept back all of the souls of our people who have

died this year. We also ask her to protect all of the souls of our ancestors."

Bridget proceeded to thank all of the spirits and the pantheon of the deity. This was one of the few important gatherings where Cessair did not take the lead; she instead stood back and awaited her turn to speak. The ceremony was long, and the attention of many was starting to drift when it became time for Bridget to announce.

"And now that the sun is setting on this year, I will formally end the marriage agreements of those couples who have decided to separate."

Bridget then listed the names of the people who no longer wished to remain married. Marriage agreements, just like the recently departed souls, had to stay 'alive' until they all could be released at the end of the year. There was always a buzz within the assembled crowd to confirm who was separating and those who may be available for new connections in the future.

The sun was finally disappearing under the horizon, signalling the end of the year and prompting Cessair's cue to speak.

"Now, with the setting sun commencing this New Year, we now start our first full year as the people of Ériu."

There was a tumultuous roar from the crowd after the earlier maudlin atmosphere of death, end and loss faded along with the afterglow of the setting sun. In its place, there was a fresh sense of the rebirth of the world and anticipation that in just six more weeks, Tabiti willing, the length of the days should again start to increase. This was the time for people to forge new marriages and alliances, plan for the year ahead, prepare for spring and new life, to embrace their annual rebirth and future with all of their soul and being. Cessair displayed a broad smile as she continued.

*"Many of us... Many of **us**... have agreed to start this year with a marriage agreement. Fintan and I..."*

Cessair's first Grand Council in Ériu.

The rest of her words were lost when another roar, even louder than the last, drowned them out. Only fragments of words and phrases shouted by the crowd could be recognised.

"About time... Fintan ...one of us...couple...future of Ériu."

The formality was over, and the New Year festivities had begun.

The following six weeks were spent preparing for the next important date in their annual calendar.

Almost every early morning, Bridget was to be found on the top of a hill that lay close to where the River Suir and the River Barrow met. She and many of the other druids had cleared the area all around the hilltop to give an unobstructed view in all directions. In the very centre, at the highest point, they manoeuvred a large stone with a sharply pointed top. There were many straight wooden poles around this stone, from the East to the South to the West. They were buried at one end in the ground, and the other end was pointing straight up.

She and her fellow druids had established and visited this site from the second day that they had set foot in Ériu. They had seen the hill when they first arrived in the ships as they sailed up the Barrow and then turned into the Suir; the hill was perfect for what they wanted. There were now some druids who lived on the hill permanently. They were there to protect it and to erect new poles as necessary.

Fintan had returned upriver, as there was still much to build around his new settlement. They had already built houses for shelter, but now they were building extra buildings for stores or animal houses. Ladra had also left; he had gone to Wexford and was repairing and maintaining the fleet of ships ready for the coming year.

Cessair, like her grandfather, when they were back in Affreidg, found she was travelling between all three villages sorting out problems. She had always started her day when the sun rose, and, in the winter, she knew that she had to make the best of the daylight.

This morning, however, it was not the sun that greeted her first, but it was her friend Bridget. Cessair had travelled, in the dark, along the now well-worn path, to the odd stone erected on the top of the hill. As she approached the rock, she saw a figure she recognised, highlighted by the predawn glow coming from the east.

"Hello, Cessair, that is you – isn't it?"

Bridget's voice cut through the still air.

"Yes! I thought I would come up and see if you can tell yet. This is such an important day for our new tribe."

Cessair could see that Bridget was concentrating on her task at hand, and as the timing was critical, she did not want to distract her. In a hushed tone, Bridget said.

"Come quickly, come here next to me and watch."

Cessair walked up and stood behind her, then looked over her head. Bridget was bent over, lining up the top of the pointed stone with a straight pole that was being held vertically, some thirty paces away. Bridget was signalling with her arms while she shouted out orders to a couple of druids some metres away.

"Left a bit, more, a bit more ... ...wait, there... that's perfect."

Just as she said those last words, Cessair saw that the sun had just started to appear from over the horizon. The two girls then walked over to where the new pole was being accurately set into the ground.

When they arrived at the pole, Cessair noticed a line of poles in an arc around the central stone. Furthermore, the distance between each pole became less and less, with the most recent being placed so close to the previous pole that it almost touched. Bridget explained.

Cessair's first Grand Council in Ériu.

"Each day the sun rises later and later, it also rises further and further around this arc of poles. When the sun reaches the end of the arc, we will have the shortest day of the year. The next day the sun will rise slightly earlier and will not reach the end pole; we will then know that the sun and the spring are coming back."

Cessair had seen similar rings in Egypt but had never seen one being built before. She then asked.

"When will the sun start to return and the days begin to lengthen?

"Tomorrow, I think. The poles are now being set so close together; that is an excellent sign. The poles over there show that the setting sun poles are also very close together. Yes! We will arrange our tribute and prayers for dawn tomorrow."

Said a very confident Bridget.

Now that the tribe had split. Only the Waterford clan members at the top of the monument hill watched the sunrise the following day.

"How does she know when the sun will start to return? How does she learn this from the gods?"

Asked Banba of Cessair in a hushed whisper. Cessair just smiled as she said.

"She is a mighty and knowledgeable druid!"

The pronouncement that the sun was returning to Ériu lifted everybody's spirits. The other villages were relayed the great news within hours of that dawn, and everyone's thoughts turned to the return of spring. Tabiti must have been happy with their preparations over the last six weeks since their new year started. She was returning the sun as a reward for their efforts, and a new cycle of life was reconfirmed for another year.

The significance of this, Tabiti's gift of light, heat, and life, was even more critical as it was also an endorsement that the Ancients approved of the settlement of Ériu.

Cessair was pleased to share the long, cold winter nights with Fintan. She now had someone to share, not just her bed but also her future. The prospect of the return of longer days, warmer days, and the new growth of spring followed by the new birth of animals and her people all helped to raise her spirit of optimism and faith in the future of Ériu.

"The cycle of life is a truly wonderful thing.
Tabiti must be respected and praised!"

The Spring brings New Growth to Ériu.

The Spring brings New Growth to Ériu.

The wolves became much bolder during the lean winter months, and attacks were all too frequent. The three settlements all suffered losses of animals, and in one case, a tribe member was badly mauled before he was rescued in the nick of time. The wolves at the start had no fear of people and just saw them as an easy meal. However, the wolves did not count on spears, daggers, or bows and arrows, and many of them learnt of such weapons with their lives. It did not take them long for the rest of the wolves to know that groups of humans should not be tackled. The humans, on the other hand, learned to build palisades to surround and protect their settlements and animals. An uneasy truce was quickly established, and both sets of sentient beings avoided each other's packs where possible.

Wolves aside, all of the villages made great progress in preparing the land to sow their precious seeds, and all celebrated the longer days and the onset of spring. It was not long until Bridget sent word to Cessair that the spring equinox would be celebrated in two days.

The two annual equinoxes, when the length of the night and the day were the same, the Winter Solstice, the shortest day and the Summer Solstice, the longest day, were four pivotal dates in the druid's year. The four dates halfway between the main four were of slightly less importance but still celebrated. The grand council would meet during the autumn equinox, but the Day of the Dead or the end of the year would occur midway between the Autumn Equinox and the Winter Solstice. All eight dates were the metronome to which the everyday farming work was scheduled.

Two days later, all of the leaders were back in Waterford, discussing the year ahead.

"The seas of winter are calming down, and with the longer days, we are ready to head back to Troy. We need to be on our way."

Ladra had a slight edge in his voice. He had been too long in one place on the land and needed to be back at sea. Cessair knew that the sea was his true home and that he missed it, and he became restless when he was not there. Cessair's attention was restored when Ladra continued.

"There are still many thousands of people to bring to Ériu. Several trips will have to be made each year for the next few years to bring them all over from Troy. Where do you want me to bring them to?"

"Bring them all to Waterford first." Said Cessair.

The Spring brings New Growth to Ériu.

Bridget, the ordinarily placid druid, was a little agitated and keen to make her point.

"When Ladra took us around Ériu, there were two places that we must inhabit as soon as possible. The spirits were truly screaming at us to settle there; I had never seen such movements from my merkhet as I did there. We must follow the spirits and settle there as quickly as possible."

Cessair's original plan was to bring everyone to Waterford and for the tribes to spread out, following the rivers from there. But the prospect of two or three thousand new people arriving each year would disrupt the local tribes that were already starting to become established. Now, with Bridget's strong request to establish two new areas as guided by the spirits, her plans changed. She turned to Ladra and spoke.

"Send most of your fleet ahead to Troy to collect the next tribes who want to come here.

Ladra, we need to learn more about Ériu, and the best way to do this is to explore her from the coast and travel up her rivers.

We also need you and some of your ships to move some of our people to the two sites that the spirits have invited us to. We will establish there two new settlements to which the new tribes that arrive can first settle and then move inland from."

Ladra was a little disappointed not to be going back to Troy immediately but was happy to discover more about the seas around Ériu. However, he did raise one concern.

"If I am not going with the fleet returning to Troy, how will they know where to bring the new tribes to?"

Cessair was quick with her response.

"Remember Kallisti in Sardinia? Remember how they used fires to guide the ships into the harbour? We will keep a fire lit close to every settlement on the coast. Just tell the captains to look out for fires or smoke to find the right place."

Bridget was delighted that Cessair should act so quickly and so decisively. Furthermore, she was excited to explore further the powerful responses that she had seen with her merkhet. She then made one more request of Cessair.

"I would ask that you settle the tribes from Egypt in the special site on this coast. I know many of them, and their experience in building in Giza would be beneficial. Furthermore, it is closer to our site here in Waterford, and I can more easily go to both."

Fintan then surprised everyone with his first words.

"I found gold in all three rivers around us. The Nore had the most. I will have to follow this river up to see where gold comes from. I gathered enough, however, to make this ring."

Fintan then presented the first gold found in Ériu to Cessair, his leader and wife, as a gesture and as a gift.

"It's beautiful; I love it. How did you find the gold?"

Asked Cessair as she attached the ring to the plaited hemp string that hung around her neck. This necklace, which had kept her precious tiger's tooth close to her heart for all these years, would now carry two precious emblems of love.

"It was slow but quite easy. I took a dish and scooped up some silt and small stones from the river. I let the water flow over the dish wash more and more of the silt away until I was left with the stones

The Spring brings New Growth to Ériu.

*and the heavy and bright gold glimmering at the bottom of the pan.
I then threw away the stones and kept the pieces of gold."*

The gold was a high-value product for Ériu and a thoughtful gift
as well.

Fintan continued,

*"I have also found large areas of rock from which we can make
copper metal; there is a great deal of metal in this rock. This copper
will be of great value to us. We can smelt it, as there is plenty of
wood to burn. We heat the rocks until the copper melts and flows
out.*

*Partholon will be very interested in trading this metal as it is
very valuable. I have brought samples of these rocks for the captains
to give to him in Troy."*

Within days, Ladra's fleet was assembled, loaded, and ready to
split and go their separate ways. The bulk of the fleet that was
heading for Troy would not be back for two or three months; the time
for the trip depended on the weather. The ships heading north just
needed to create two new settlements in time to settle the new tribes
when they arrived.

Ladra again only took two ships. During the winter, he had made
many smaller boats, each capable of navigating the smaller rivers.
Each boat could carry up to ten people up any river; these were towed
behind the ships while they were at sea.

It took less than two days to reach the mouth of the river for the
first site that Bridget had identified. Ladra guided his ships up the
tidal bit of the river while some of his passengers continued upriver
in the smaller boats. Progress was slow as the river flowed quickly
and was still swollen with the winter rains. Bridget was visibly
excited and demanded to be set ashore at regular intervals so she

could 'consult' her merkhet. These frequent stops were starting to annoy the rowers, who were just beginning to get into a rhythm when they were repeatedly told to stop. Again and again, this happened, so much so that Cessair whispered to Fintan.

"Head druid or not, how long do you think before these rowers will 'accidentally' throw her in the river?"

Fintan's response also whispered was,

"How long before I throw her in!

They had not travelled much longer when Bridget did not climb on board after one of her consultations. She beckoned Cessair and Fintan to follow her up the hill heading away from the river. They walked up the gentle slope until Bridget announced.

"We have arrived! This is the place. I have never, ever sensed the spirits so strongly as I do here, now."

Cessair looked around and was surprised at the view. The river curved around the small hill that they were standing on. Looking up, she could see the best dry lands for miles in most directions; they were ideal for farming. But most of all, even Cessair could 'feel' that this place was special and that she too was part of it.

Fintan went down to tell the rest of the people in the boats to set up camp close to the river. He sent back the boatmen to the ships to collect the rest of the passengers. Looking back up the hill, he saw Cessair and Bridget deep in conversation.

Bridget consulted her merkhet many times, and every time she made some new revelation to Cessair. Too excited to fully explain her findings, but enough to let Cessair know that this place was special. Finally, Bridget slowed down, took a great breath, let it out slowly and said.

The Spring brings New Growth to Ériu.

"This must be one of the most important sites in the world! My people coming from Giza would not believe me if I told them everything. They need to find out about this place for themselves. We must settle close by here and keep this place holy for the spirits. Please, we must call it Sí an Bhrú? Exceptional spirits live here."

It was not long before a stream of people climbed the slope to see what was so interesting. Cessair left Bridget to tell everyone about what she had sensed, and Cessair went back down to talk to Fintan.

"That is one happy druid. I hope she finds the next site as exciting."

Fintan laughed and spoke.

"She is a changed woman since she arrived in Ériu."

"We all are!"

Countered Cessair as the pair explored the riverbank.

While the village was being built, Ladra returned to Waterford to pick up two more boatloads of people. He returned a week later to find the settlement well started with many houses already built. Bith had travelled with the second wave of people and was impressed with the site and house-building progress. The winds had become too strong for sea travel, so the ships were safely harboured in the shelter of the river estuary. The following week everybody built together, and the new village advanced well.

The weather improved, so Cessair led half of the people back to the ships, and they, once more, progressed up the coast to the next chosen site. Cessair was glad that her father was with them for this next stage of their journey. She had planned to stop with the people who made the axes on the island in the north, and she wanted her father's experience in diplomacy. Bridget did not want to leave the new important site, but Cessair had to insist saying.

"Did you not say that the other side of the island was also very important? I need you to find the sites on the west side where the spirits will also accept us."

Bridget could not argue with her own words, and so she somewhat reluctantly joined the 'away' party and left **her** new important spiritual centre on the banks of the River Bóinne.

The Fusion of Two Cultures.

The island of the people who made the axes was small. But as it was not far from the north coast of Ériu, it was not hard to find. The island was only a few miles across. It was shaped like a boomerang with a small, protected harbour and a well-sheltered deep-water bay. Both were protected by the curve of the land on either side.

As they had reached the north of Ériu, the great ocean waves could reach the travellers, and they rocked and pitched Ladra's ships until most of the passengers became queasy, and some were very sick. The good natural harbour on the south side of the island gave some protection from the westerly waves, and everyone was glad of the opportunity to steady themselves and to prepare themselves to meet the island's inhabitants. Once docked, everyone was happy that they had arrived and once again could stand on safe, dry land.

All of the islanders had lined the pier. They had seen the ships as they approached from the east. They were used to traders coming and going, but these two ships looked different.

The islanders were armed but not aggressive; they were cautious and more than a little alarmed. The sight of two large ships full of people just turning up at their pier would have worried anyone not alone in a small, isolated island community with nowhere to run. Trading ships only carried a minimum crew; these ships were different. Why should so many people be on board?

Standing out at the front was a large, heavyset man who was obviously their leader. He was well-aged, and he must have had a hard life by the look of his weather-beaten, deeply lined face and somewhat ruddy complexion. He was a giant of a man whose massive physic would have matched Balor's. Cessair surprised herself by thinking of Balor, but this man's sheer size was only ever compared, in her experience, by Balor.

"Have you ever seen a man with such big hands?"

Whispered Cessair to her father as they disembarked and went to meet the stranger. Ladra and Bridget followed closely behind. There was visible relief when the islander recognised Ladra from his earlier visit, and the whole mood of all of the islanders changed rapidly.

"We are so pleased to see you; my name is Angus."

These were the first words spoken by their leader as he moved forward to greet Ladra and his company.

The Fusion of Two Cultures.

*"You will be here for a few days. That is only the start of the
rough sea."*

Angus raised an upright hand in the direction of the large waves
as though he was beckoning them to stop.

*"A storm is coming, and the sea will not be safe for any man, no
matter how big your ships are. You are welcome to camp here. You
must shelter your boats over there in that cove, away from the worst
of the waves. Be quick now; you will not have much time as the
weather and sea change very quickly here."*

No sooner than he had finished those words, then the boats
started to pitch and bang dangerously against the pier. It did not take
much time to unload the ships and move them to safer waters, but
even then, it was just in time. Only minutes later, one large rogue
wave crashed into the pier and almost destroyed it. Ladra just stood
back and watched, dumbfounded. He knew that that wave would
have severely damaged one, if not both, of his ships! He never saw
the sea change so quickly before; he had just learnt something else
about Ériu. Bridget also realised that she had a great deal to learn
about Manandan.

With everyone off the two ships, there was a large number of
Cessair's people encamped on the island. With well-rehearsed
precision, a small town grew in less than an hour. Fires were lit, food
was being cooked, tents were erected and furnished, and even music
was played. They had been told that they had to wait out the stormy
seas for a few days, so they settled in for the duration. With so many
strangers, once again, Cessair could sense a tension in their host's
demeanour, and so she asked her father to invite Angus and his
family to come over for a meal in her tent.

Whether it was a mistake in understanding or the natural
curiosity of the islanders was never known, but shortly afterwards,
every available man, woman and child accepted the invitation.

Seeing so many people descending on her camp en-bloc even alarmed Cessair at first, but her worries evaporated when she saw that they were carrying gifts, not weapons. This was Santorini all over again, and once again, everyone was in the mood to make new friends and have some fun.

There were some language problems, but the islanders were used to some traders and their different tongues. With the aid of some of Bith's fermented juice and an equivalent island brew, both sides understood each other well enough.

"Thank you!"

Said Angus as he and a few of his family sat down around the fire at Cessair's tent.

"I have never met a leader so young before."

He did not add, *'and a woman',* which greatly pleased Cessair. She liked Angus, and she had a good feeling that they could become good allies. Angus continued.

"Most of our people came here from the land over the sea."

He pointed towards the land that could just be seen some miles to the east. He was pointed towards the larger sister island to Ériu.

"My ancestors came from there; most of us were born here. Other of our ancestors were fishermen taken north by the sea from a country very far to the south. Also, a few people from the trading ships have stayed and joined us."

Bith asked the strategically important question.

"Are there any other tribes living close by, on the mainland of Ériu?"

Angus let out a big hearty laugh and spoke.

The Fusion of Two Cultures.

"Ériu! I like that name. It suits that land. No! There are no tribes living close by. There is, however, one small tribe that lives well down the next big river to the west. During the summer, they live in a place where that river heads towards a small inland sea. It is more like a hunting camp than a village."

Cessair was pleased to hear about those who were living close by and of their histories. She thought that Angus would like to hear about a little of her immediate history, so she started.

"We were peaceful farmers living many, many miles away to the east. Our lands became flooded when our old sea god attacked our country Affreidg, and many thousands of us had to run for our lives."

"Was that about ten years ago?

Interrupted Angus.

"About eight years now! We built a town called Troy...

Angus again interrupted Cessair.

"Yes, we have heard of Troy and Affreidg and of the great flood. The Sherden regularly come here, and they have told us all about your tribe. How you are growing food and have invented so many new ways of doing things and making new materials. I have also heard about you going to Egypt and...

Cessair sat silently, listening to the history that she was going to tell him. There were many minor mistakes, but the main story was correct. She could not be anything but impressed at his world knowledge on this remote, tiny island in the endless sea. She also felt great pride that she and her tribes were worthy of world news status. It was a full ten minutes before Angus drew his long monologue to a close with the words.

"...there is so much that we want to learn about your new ways."

This scene in Cessair's tent was repeated right across the whole makeshift village of tents that night. A great many new friendships were made, and the few language problems simply faded away.

Early the following day, the sun was out, and it was dry, but there was still a strong wind, and the waves were still wild. Fintan and Cessair were alone, standing high up on the cliffs, a long way above the sea. They were mesmerised at the power of Manandan and of his great waves crashing onto the rocks so far below. But even at this great height, the sea spray rose to greet them in Manandan's wet embrace.

Cessair's mind flashed back all those years ago when she and her young friends looked down on the silver thread that was the River Danube and discussed another god. Her thoughts then turned to Dana, and she instinctively reached for the tooth that hung around her neck.

"Impressive sight. We call it the Atlantic Ocean. The land as we know it is all held up by it.

Good morning."

Cessair was brought back from her reverie by Angus' warm greeting. Angus did not wait for a reply but continued.

"The sea will be rough all day. You will be my guests today, and I will show you around my island. Come follow me."

Without even waiting for a reply, the big man had turned on his heel and was striding off uphill towards the heart of the island. Cessair and Fintan just looked at each other and then followed Angus before he disappeared too far ahead. Despite Angus being at least a generation older than his young guests, it did not take long before he had to stop and wait for them to catch up. The mountainous terrain and long heather were difficult to cross for those not used to the small animal pathways and tracks. While their path was difficult, what kept the duo behind was their constant admiration of the spectacular views that appeared around every corner or crest.

The clouds above them had somewhere important to go, and they were in no mood to wait. As they passed overhead, their shadows chased after them across the more difficult path on the ground; they were desperately trying to keep up. It was as though both were fleeing from the terrible wrath of the sea that had been chasing them and was now crashing against the cliffs behind them with its furious roar. Manandan was angry that the clouds had stolen some of his water, and he wanted it back. The spirits of the clouds were laughing and skipping across the sky; they were out of his reach, and they were taunting him. They knew that they had now made it to land, and even their shadows were now out of his clutches. From their high vantage point, Cessair and Fintan often stopped to watch the different spirits at their sport. They appreciated how the superior sun projected the cloud's antics upon the mottled screen of the land and sea far below them.

Angus was stopped at a large hole in the side of the hill and speaking to some people working there. When the duo arrived, they saw that inside the large gash in the hillside was an area of black and shiny rock. Several men were breaking this rock into large fist-size stones.

"This is where we collect the stones for our axes. That huge slab of shiny rock is where our axes come from. We use other stones as hammers to break off the pieces that we will work with. Then we chip off small pieces with other stones to roughly shape the axe. Then we take the crudely shaped head back to our village for the next work that we will do to it."

Angus had just finished his well-rehearsed talk and was about to move on with his tour when Cessair asked.

"How long have your people been making axes here?

Angus was surprised to be asked any questions about his people, even simple ones. For decades the usual traders typically just wanted to be on their way back home quickly. They were usually highly secretive and tried to talk as little as possible beyond the selling points of the axes. They just wanted to be able to go and sell their newly bought wares at significant profits. Here, on this tour, there was someone interested and wanted to learn about his people, not just the product.

"We have been here for hundreds of generations. Life is hard here, and many die, but we also have many new people joining us from different parts of the world. Our axes sell well, and we live well because of them."

Angus surprised himself with how he had opened up to these new people of Ériu. The secretive wall, essential in business trading, was gone, and they were all just people, just trying to learn from each other and help each other with their daily lives.

The Fusion of Two Cultures.

It was a long walk back to Angus' village, and he constantly asked about the laws in Ériu and how their society was structured there. Just as they were all entering the village, they saw a man that was tied to a stake with a strong rope, and he could not move far. Angus pointed to the man and said.

"That man only joined us here at the end of last year. He is lazy, does not work, and he just steals what he wants. A few days ago, a fisherman tried to stop him from stealing his fish. The fisherman was attacked and hurt so that he could not work. I have punished this bad man by tying him up there for a few weeks with no shelter, minimal food, or water to try and stop him from behaving badly again.

Cessair, what would you do with him in Ériu?"

She thought for a moment and said.

"His bad deed has hurt three people and the tribe. The fisherman cannot work, and the tribe has no fish. The man watching him and tending to him also cannot produce any axes for the tribe. The thief cannot work either and is just building revenge against the tribe for his punishment, pain, and isolation. In all cases, your people lose.

In Ériu, there is no prison, but the thief must work to minimise the harm that he has done. In this case, he must do the fishing for the fisherman until the fisherman is well and then still do a little more fishing for free; the tribe still gets fish. The thief has the dignity of producing something and learns not to be so lazy."

Angus was impressed by her answer but still asked.

"But what if the thief refuses to work or help the fisherman, or he just steals again?"

Cessair's answer was simple but harsh.

"He is then banished from the tribe.

Everyone in the tribe must help each other to their best ability – we each take pride in that. But if this man does not want to follow the tribe rules and be a part of our tribe, then he must take his chances alone, outside of the tribe, with only the wolves for company."

The trio had now reached Angus' village, and they had stopped beside a woman who was working on an axe head. Angus restarted his tour talk.

"This woman takes one of the crudely chipped and shaped stones; she wets the big flat stone in front of her, and then she rubs the roughly formed axe against the flat stone. In time the axe head becomes smooth as it is polished, and a sharp edge is formed at the end. It takes many days of polishing to make one sharp axe head."

Fintan lifted a finished axe and was impressed with how smooth and shiny it was and how sharp the finished stone edge could be. He turned back to Angus and asked.

"These axes are perfect, and we could use them to clear around our new sites. What can we swap with you to purchase these axes?"

Angus was ready with his reply as he was expecting the question and was keen to trade as his people were running very short of one commodity.

"We need more clay pots and vessels. Do you have any to spare? The few we already have are those we traded some time ago, and many are now broken."

Fintan looked down, slightly saddened, and answered.

The Fusion of Two Cultures.

"We have very few on board our ships and only have what we use. I will look. We may have a few."

Cessair then asked Angus.

"Why do you not make them?

Angus' answer surprised both Cessair and Fintan.

"We don't know how!"

It was then apparent to both Fintan and Cessair why the foreign traders were so secretive. They were swapping valuable axes that took many days to make for pots that only took a few hours to complete.

Cessair was annoyed that the traders had taken such advantage of Angus and his people. Life was hard enough, she thought, and there was no need to make life even harder by not sharing new technology or making equitable swops.

"We do not have many new pots to share with you, but we will show you how to make them for yourselves. We have been making them for hundreds of generations back in Affreidg, and for us, they are not hard to make. You say that it will be a few days before we can safely put to sea and continue our journey; we will use that time to teach you how to make pots."

Angus was genuinely excited and rushed off to call some of his people's elders and best craftsmen. Fintan also went off to collect several of his tribe who were particularly good at making pots.

Cessair just sat down and started to talk about everything and nothing with the axe grinders, and she found them to be uncharacteristically pleasant with little to complain about.

A short time later, there was quite a crowd amassed and an expectant buzz within the islander group. Like a teacher, Fintan was in his element and addressed them all.

"Break up into small groups of three or four. The islanders must take our people to all the places where they have clay. Our people know what they are looking for, and they will teach your people what clay is best. The clay must be smooth enough to be rolled out between your hands without falling apart."

A few minutes later, Cessair was almost alone, with only a few of the remaining islanders to keep her company. She enjoyed doing nothing, for a change, other than talking with new friends from a different culture.

It was almost dark when the clay 'treasure hunters' all returned. Many were carrying great bags of candidate clay. A shallow hole had been dug in the ground, and a fire was lit at the bottom. There was plenty of space around the fire to gently dry pots as they were made. This was before the later 'firing' that would be necessary. Fintan then continued his master class with dozens of eager students of all ages.

"First, you must roll and knead the clay with your hands to remove all of the air bubbles. Now add two handfuls of clay to one handful of the sand or tiny broken pieces left over from making your axes. Mix it thoroughly with no air bubbles, roll and knead it again. Take a round stone, put slippery grease or animal fat on it and cover half of it with the clay mix. Then pat it all around with a flat stick to beat out any remaining air. When you have your shape formed and smooth, remove the stone. You should normally leave it for a few weeks to dry slowly. Today we will rush the process, and because of that, tomorrow, many of the pots may well crack. Now set them around the fire so they will slowly dry. Turn them around regularly

to dry them evenly, as we have not left them for weeks. Warming them down in this hole will stop a gust of wind from cooling the clay rapidly and cracking it. Leave them close to the fire; someone must keep it lit all night. Tomorrow, we will fire them to turn them into stone hard pots."

Fintan spoke in almost total silence. No one wanted to miss a precious word that he was saying. At the end of his lesson, food was presented, music started and yet again a party atmosphere developed around the kiln fire. Both leaders looked around, and they were pleased that the two groups of people, from very different cultures, were completely intermingled and fully united.

The following day Fintan resumed his lesson to a large crowd of eager islanders. All were keen to see how to make these precious pots.

"Now, yesterday's pots are all dry and too hot to touch. We now fire them. I will add fresh dry wood on top of the hot ashes and all around the dried pots."

Fintan now carefully placed extra dry wood all around the pots and filled the hole in the ground with timber. Soon the hole in the ground became a large pile of wood with pots and fire at the bottom.

"Watch as the flames burn hotter and hotter, and the pots become covered with white hot ashes."

The fire raged for several hours before it started to die down. Fintan instructed that the fire or the pots should not be touched for two days or until it was cool enough for someone to reach in with their bare hands.

The following day the sea had calmed down, and Cessair was ready to move on. She decided, however, to wait for the extra day to allow Fintan to finish his pottery lesson being given to their newfound friends.

All of the islanders were huddled around the fire pit. They were talking excitedly, trying to guess if the pots were good. They became silent as Fintan sifted through the spent ashes to retrieve the new pots. He gently removed the ash from around the first pot. He did so just as carefully as any archaeologist would do thousands of years later. The first pot lifted out whole, and a huge cheer went up. Fintan flicked the rim with his fingernail, and the pot fell apart. The cheer was replaced by a wave of disappointed *'Awws.'*

The Fusion of Two Cultures.

The next pot, a large one, also came out whole, but there were fewer cheers this time. Fintan lifted the pot up high and again flicked it with his fingernail.

"DING!"

It chimed like a bell.

"Hurrah!"

Was the crowd's response as Fintan handed it over to a delighted Angus – the first-ever clay pot had now been made on their island. About half of the pots made were good and had no cracks. Fintan told them that next time, they should not rush the early drying stage and that almost all of the pots would be good and useful.

The islanders, in the past, would have traded the few pots made in those three days for three months of hard, axe-making work. Foreign traders would now have to pay a higher price if they wanted Angus' precious axes.

"We now have great allies in those islanders."

Cessair said to Ladra as they sailed away the following day.

"They gave us a whole pile of axes for Fintan's lessons, and they refused any further payment of any kind."

The stop on the island delayed the coastal expedition, but all agreed that the time there was very well spent. They followed the coast west past the great river, which the hunting tribe lived on, then south and then west again. They travelled on making a mental note of all the places that they would need to visit someday. It was well into the second day when Bridget excitedly said.

"We are very close; we must stop soon!"

The Merkhet Speaks Again.

The ships followed their course for over an hour, moving parallel to the coast but always going west. There were high cliffs with the land behind gently rising to the low mountains some miles off. The land looked fertile, with large expanses of lightly wooded grassland leading to heavier timbers on the slopes of the distant hills.

Strangely, the whole area reminded everyone of Affreidg. It was hard to say in what way this land ashore was familiar to so many on board, but most agreed that it *felt like home.*' Soon Bridget was not the only one who wanted to land and investigate.

The ships continued west, and Bridget and her merkhet became increasingly excited with every passing minute. The agitation in the instrument was reflected in the druid that held it. She just had to stop, stand on dry land, and test her instrument of knowing without the ship's movement. Ladra, on the other hand, could not find a sheltered and safe place to stop. Some way back, there had been a sandy bay, but the large Atlantic rolling waves made landing too risky. The sea was too deep to anchor, and if they tried to anchor close to the shore, the waves were just too big. Much to Bridget's annoyance, the ships sailed on.

Just as the merkhet response started to fade once more, Ladra saw what looked like a river estuary; he then turned the ships and sailed inland. Ladra dropped the sails, but the ships continued to be carried along by the incoming tide. The water was deep and reasonably wide, so he allowed the tide to dictate his route and carry the ships onward and inland.

He saw what looked like another small river on his left. It headed back towards where Bridget said she wanted to land; he made a mental note to use the small boats for that trip.

Cessair then shouted out.

The Merkhet Speaks Again.

"Look! Look over there. There! High up on the cliffs, standing on that headland; don't you see it?"

Everyone in the party immediately looked up, but no one else saw the great stag that had been so clear to her. She started to explain but then realised that she, just like her father before her, had received a personal message directly from the spirit of Ériu.

The ships continued inland until they entered a huge natural harbour. All around were low hills covered with mature trees and some open areas of grassland. Small streams flowed down from the hills carrying a bountiful supply of fresh water. Ladra was almost as excited as Bridget had been earlier; she just sat annoyed that they could not have stopped earlier when her merkhet had 'spoken' the loudest.

"This is the best natural harbour that I have ever seen."

Said Ladra to an unappreciative and captive audience who just wanted to stand steady on the dry land. He went on.

"This is a broad haven that would shelter any number of our ships in the roughest of the winter storms. Manandan has guided us here; this is the perfect port for any ship or even a fleet of ships."

The mention of Manandan brought Bridget's and the rest of the companies' attention to the importance of this safe harbour. They were all glad to be out of the big rolling Atlantic waves.

After her own private and spiritual invitation by Ériu's great Elk, Cessair just said.

"This place is perfect; our new settlement will use it as its harbour. We will call it 'Broadhaven.' We will make camp at the bottom of that small ridge today, and tomorrow we will split up into small groups and explore the whole area, with each party going in different directions."

The camp was quickly set up, and plans were made for the next day. There was great excitement that night in the camp; everyone knew this place was also special. The sea here was well sheltered, and the Broadhaven waters were tucked away, safe from any possible Atlantic violence. All around them, there were forests of excellent trees on the slopes of gentle hills. It was as though the spirits of Ériu were just waiting to welcome the new settlers.

Cessair lay down tired that night, ready for a good night's sleep. But just as she was about to fall asleep, she focussed on Fintan's soft breathing beside her. She softly spoke to him, not even knowing whether or not he was sleeping.

"You know, even in this small tent, this is the first time since we left Affreidg all those years ago that I have truly felt at home."

Fintan never answered, but instead, she heard the quite friendly whispers of the local spirits that were being gently carried to her across the still night air.

Cessair was not up at dawn as she usually would have been; she had slept in! This was so rare that Fintan even returned to their tent and asked.

"Cessair! Are you well? Is something wrong? Why are you still lying in bed? Your breakfast is ready outside."

She smiled and looked up at Fintan.

"Everything is just perfect. Thank you. I am coming now. Oh! I am not very hungry."

By the time Cessair joined the rest of the tribe outside, everyone was very busy. She went in search of Fintan but could not find him anywhere. She saw Bith and Bridget, who were gathering supplies and loading two of the smaller access boats. They were going with a dozen others to explore the small river that they had passed as they entered Broadhaven. The river seemed to lead back in the direction of where Bridget's merkhet had reacted so violently. Bith also wanted to head back in that direction as he had seen, from the ship, a large expanse of land that would be quickly cleared for crops and animals.

She saw Ladra, who was exploring Broadhaven bay. The place had so much going for it. He had to find out what areas dried at low tide, where there were underwater rocks that could damage his ships, or even just work out the best place to build a pier and still have deep water to float at low tide.

The two ships had brought many people to Broadhaven, but except for Cessair, everyone was busy. Many were just doing routine support work, such as gathering or preparing food, while others were preparing to set off and explore the surrounding area.

It was not very long before she saw Fintan returning from the south. As he approached, an excited Fintan called out to Cessair.

"Come with me! Just to the top of this slope behind me. It will not take long."

Cessair joined Fintan, and they both walked up the slope that was a ridge of slightly higher ground gently rising behind their camp.

When she reached the top, she first looked south, but all she saw was more sea. Then she saw the land on the east, which she expected, and then she saw land on the west also going south. The sea was completely calm, so it could not be the Atlantic. It must be another, much larger bay.

"This ridge of land must be the only access to all that land in the west as that sea down there in front of us just had to come in somewhere. Look, this ridge that we are standing on becomes very narrow over there; that land beyond is almost an island. We must explore it today; reaching the end can't be too far away."

As they were walking back to their tent, they saw Ladra preparing a small team to survey Broadhaven's waters. He had been looking for any excuse to get back into a boat, even a small one. He knew that his ships were moored up and that they would not be going anywhere for a few weeks. He also did not want to travel overland, on foot, to explore the internal lands. He was not lazy; in fact, just the contrary, he rarely stopped. His childhood passion had become an obsession – he just loved to be on the water! He might as well learn about Broadhaven before he started making it into his new giant harbour.

Fintan thought that he would tease Ladra a little with the words.

"Not like you, Ladra, to pass up a chance to explore new areas."

Ladra looked up, a little surprised. Surely Fintan knew he hated tramping through long grass or forests or even climbing local hills. So, he simply replied without being drawn into any justifications.

"I am leaving the exploring to you, and I am preparing a plan for our new harbour."

Fintan continued.

"Cessair and I are exploring the land to the west. We are going south down the Atlantic coast."

Ladra thought for a moment; he then replied.

"Thanks, but I will wait for a few days and then explore the coast by ship."

He ended with the quip.

"Much easier than walking."

Fintan was now ready for the end of his little tease, but even then, he would bury it in his careful choice of words. He wanted Ladra to work for the little bit of information that would make him abandon his imminent harbour plans. He continued in a deliberately indifferent tone; he wondered if Ladra was even really listening.

"We will follow the Atlantic coast south and then return up the peninsular on the west coast. We will then return across the isthmus that is the ridge behind our camp."

Sure enough, Ladra was just about to reply with an apathetic comment when he stopped for a second. He abandoned his boat and headed up the ridge as he repeated quietly but still out loud.

"Peninsula...... West Coast .... Isthmus??"

Fintan and Cessair both laughed as Ladra ran up the ridge, and he was soon gone. Fintan turned to Cessair and said.

"He will never forgive us for finding this large, sheltered, important sea inlet before him. It is so close to our camp, and he so prides himself on being the local expert on everything related to the sea, yet he never even knew it was just over that ridge!"

Not long later, all of the exploring parties met up briefly before setting off in different directions. Bith and Bridget's team would be away for a few days as they were to travel the furthest. Cessair's should be back relatively quickly, but they would still bring tents and supplies anyway.

The four exploratory teams all set off around the same time. They were leaving about half of the settlement to collect supplies and establish a more permanent Broadhaven harbour settlement. As they were going, Cessair asked Fintan.

"Have you seen Ladra? I thought that he would have been at that meeting. He could have at least seen us off!"

"I did see him just before the meeting running around gathering people up. But since then, I have no idea where he is."

Fintan replied as they walked along the ridge heading west. As they reached the narrowest point of the isthmus, they saw a tail of

The Merkhet Speaks Again.

Broadhaven water just on their right and on their left, only 200 meters away, was the new undiscovered sandy bay. Cessair, with an almost childish glee, said.

"Let's be the first to reach that bay and claim it as our discovery. That would annoy Ladra!"

She ran ahead, leaving Fintan behind; she wanted to be the first. Not to be outdone, Fintan took up the challenge and raced after her at a great pace. He was slowly catching up with her, but she would still easily arrive on the new beach before him, even with his much longer legs. He knew that she would never stop teasing him about her winning this race.

She would have 'won' that race easily, but she had just stopped short of her goal. She was still, quiet, and staring at something just a few paces away. When Fintan caught up with her, she was still staring and silent, and he started to worry if something was wrong. He then heard a familiar voice.

"There you are! Wait up. We are coming with you."

Ladra stood on the beach with a great grin on his face. He stood next to one of the access boats and a crew of six tribe members already with their oars.

"I am so glad that I found this sea!

We will sail and row down this bay. If this gives us good access to the Atlantic, then Broadhaven is even more important with its own sheltered 'back door' for boats.

If you go down the peninsular by land, we will meet you where this bay meets the Atlantic, and then we will bring you back by boat."

Cessair and Fintan just looked at each other, exchanged a knowing smile and then agreed to meet Fintan later at the arranged point. They tried not to show any surprise at Ladra's change of heart or even the lengths that he had gone to so as not to miss out on exploring this new expanse of water.

The tide was going out, and Ladra's team kept pushing the boat further out over the sand into deeper water. A few minutes later, they were gone, rowing into deeper water and hoping for a wind in the right direction to push them south. Once they were out of earshot, Cessair and Fintan fell about laughing. Fintan spoke first.

"Typical Ladra! Determined not to be left behind with anything to do with the sea."

Cessair replied.

"When that man is 'fired up', he can move mountains. How did he move that boat overland so quickly? He certainly did not want to miss out."

*"He beat **you** to the beach, **and** he took a boat! At least I will not be teased for not reaching it before you."*

Fintan retorted, and both he and Cessair laughed at being eclipsed by Ladra's stubborn curiosity. They were in great spirits as they travelled west to meet the Atlantic coast.

It was not long until they stood again high on a cliff top, on a promontory point, looking out at the vast Atlantic.

As far as their eyes could see, there was water. From the south all the way around, through the west to the north, there was nothing but water.

"I can see why Ladra called it the Endless Sea."

Said Cessair as she took a few moments to take in its beauty.

The Merkhet Speaks Again.

"Look, Fintan, see how far in the distance the sky meets the sea. It meets in a slight curve, as though the world is bent."

Fintan was the practical voice of his time. He said.

"The sun is round, the moon is round, even the stars and planets in the sky are round. Is it not then highly likely that our world, which Tabiti also made, is also round?"

Cessair was quick to reply.

"If the world is round, then we are not at the end of the world."

Equally quickly, Fintan replied.

"We are at the edge of our world, and that is far enough!"

The duo headed south along the coast. The high cliffs soon disappeared, and the coastline changed to long stretches of sandy beaches. Sand dunes rose high above sea level and stretched some distance inland.

A strong wind blew from the sea, and it picked up small pieces of sand and blew them on top of the dunes. Here, on the top, the grass was growing, making the dunes look like small hills. Cessair and Fintan walked along the beach just above where the large Atlantic waves had crashed down and finally submitted to the dominance of the land.

Cessair turned to Fintan and said.

"I can feel Api, the land, and the sea are living and changing all of the time that we are here – Ériu is so special."

At one point, they climbed the dunes to have a better vantage point and to see where they were and what was around them. At first, the soft sand was hard to climb, but when they reached the grassed area, the rest of the way to the top was easy. They were surprised when they did reach it because instead of seeing land in front of them, they saw the waters of the bay and another large sandy beach. Here the peninsular was only a few hundred meters wide.

"Look south."

Said Fintan.

The Merkhet Speaks Again.

"The peninsular widens out again, and the trees start again. See there, far in the distance; there is a steep hill. If we climb it, we will have a great view all around us and be able to see just where we are."

The trees were not dense, but it still took the pair a few hours to reach the top of the hill.

No trees grew at the top of the hill as the winds coming from the Atlantic were too strong, and they quickly uprooted any tree that tried to establish itself there. The lack of trees meant that the views all around them were completely unobstructed and stunning.

After several minutes the ever-practical Fintan spoke first.

"We are surrounded on three sides by water. Just down there, ahead of us, is where the bay meets the sea. We have reached the end of the peninsular. That sheltered bay we found is enormous.

Cessair did not reply at first. She had heard but did not listen to Fintan's words. She just stood and looked; she turned and looked again, and again, and again. Her brain worked furiously, trying to take in and record all that was laid out before her. She found herself talking mentally to herself as she gathered her thoughts.

"That land there is in the north, close to Broadhaven. That is where we started our trip, and the large bay ends. This land here is almost surrounded by water; it has a broad tail at the top and a head at this end. It is as though it were a great fish swimming out to sea. If this end is the head, I must be standing on its eye; what a fantastic view it has."

She turned east and saw that far across the bay was more flat land, but just behind it, there was a tall range of mountains. She turned south and looked a mile or so across the bay's entrance at a line of cliffs that dropped straight down into the sea.

"What sea cliffs – I have never seen any so high or spectacular in all of my life. They are awesome."

But of all of the views, she saw that day, the view to the west truly captured her imagination. She sat down, grabbed Fintan's hand and pulled him down on the soft grass beside her.

"Just look!"

That was all that she said. At first, Fintan just saw the Atlantic with a few islands in it. But after a few minutes, the scene also spoke to his soul.

The sun was just starting to set behind a small island someway offshore. The island blocked part of the sun, and soon, it would all be lost below the sea. There was a strange light that showed everything in clear relief, yet it was a gentle light that emphasised the colours of everything. As if to orchestrate the tableau set out below them, a pair of circulating Sea Eagles called 'time' to the remains of the daylight.

The sky turned crimson red, almost a blood red, a colour that should have screamed a warning to Cessair and her companion, but this time, it just emphasised how special this place was.

Fintan urged Cessair to leave and climb down to the coast before it became completely dark. Just as she turned to leave, she took one last glance out to the west. She froze, tugged at Fintan's arm, and pointed out towards an island a mile or so offshore.

"Look at that island! Do you see it? It has a golden glow coming from its heart. A pillar of light started at that island and shafted straight up towards the heavens. There is something very special out there."

Fintan just took Cessair's hand and led her quickly downhill as the daylight had almost gone. At first, Cessair complained that she had wanted to stay, but then she agreed that the path would be treacherous in the dark and that they should hurry down the hill.

The Merkhet Speaks Again.

When they reached the hill's bottom, it was almost pitch black, as there was no moonlight that night. They were just about to make a forced camp under a small tree when Cessair espied a campfire not very far ahead. They did not want to jump to the conclusion that they had met up with Ladra and his crew, so they approached very quietly from the shadows.

Ladra and his crew were singing and in great form when Cessair and Fintan crept up on them and gave them a great scare.

"We could have attacked you before you even knew we were there. You must be more careful; there are still dangerous animals here."

Cessair scolded them, but she did not upset their great mood. She had not forgotten how Ladra had beaten her to the bay and robbed her 'victory' from Fintan.

Ladra handed Cessair and Fintan a large fish that he had just cooked on the fire.

"This fish is called a 'Mullet', and the sea is full of them, and they are easily caught. This bay is huge, well-sheltered, and full of fish and shells. Many of the shells are the type with the purple dye – there are so many of them."

Cessair remembered the view she had of the peninsular from the top of the hill just a few hours earlier. She then proclaimed.

"We will call this piece of land after this beautiful fish from this bay. We will call it 'The Beautiful Mullet.'"

They were all tired when they lay down to sleep. Cessair was glad that the following day she could be a lazy passenger while Ladra's crew would take them back to Broadhaven on the little boat.

She lay down next to Fintan but did not fall asleep immediately.

Her mind went over what she had seen that day and all of the places they had been. The day was meant to be just another exploratory mission. It was a trip to find what resources were available to the settling clans, but the day turned out to be so much more. She had experienced so many diverse human emotions, and she felt that she was in empathy with many feelings that must have come from the Ancients themselves.

Looking down from the high cliffs at the vast expanse of ocean, the ocean formed a slight curve on the horizon, making her feel small and insignificant. However, walking along the beach while holding her lover's hand, she now felt intimately aware that they were within and part of the crucible of creation and life. The roar of the great crashing waves pounding and attacking the land on one side, the warm, dry wind, which was blowing through her hair, picked up tiny grains of sand that had been broken away by Manandan's attack. The wind now used those broken soldiers to fortify the wall of sand on her left. The land plants themselves grew there to stabilise and strengthen that crucial front line.

However, what stood out, was even more memorable and intriguing. It was the island with the golden glow; it was as though it wanted her to notice it. Was it a personal invitation for her?

She was surprised at Fintan not even mentioning the island and at his taking of her hand to take her away from the top of that hill. She started to wonder if Fintan had even seen the island's golden glow at all. She then thought that maybe the golden invitation was for her only.

She made herself a promise that night that was to have great implications for the rest of her life.

"I will come back and visit that island, and I will go there sometime soon."

Life, The Universe and Everything; The Ancients.

Old Friends and Unexpected Visitors.

Once again, Ériu lived up to its name and Cessair, and her people were spoiled for choice. There was an opportunity in every direction, and every exploring party came back with great news.

Cessair knew that the Beautiful Mullet offered great fishing, dry sandy land for the winter grazing of stock and vast amounts of the tiny shells that produced the valuable dye.

Bith found that the land that they had seen from the boats was as good as they had hoped. It would be easy to clear. There was plenty of deep rich soil, and being on a gentle slope, it was well-drained and would grow crops very well. The cliff-top site was huge, went back for several miles, and was even longer along the coast. It could grow crops and grazing animals in such numbers that it would sustain and feed many thousands of settlers.

Bridget was very excited about her spirit responses and said that while they were not as strong as at the site on the other side of Ériu, they were indeed very powerful. She went on to say that the further east she went, the stronger the response she got with her merkhet. She was annoyed that they had to turn back rather than see where her merkhet led her, but she promised to return soon and to follow her pendulum to where it wanted to take her.

Another party found a large, well-sheltered freshwater lake full of great fish. It was safely nestled between two hills. This was yet another great area with potential for settlement.

Ladra had already enthused about how good a port Broadhaven could become. All the sites explored were within easy reach of Broadhaven, so Cessair decided that the first built settlement would be at Broadhaven. It could serve future settlers wanting to build at the other great local places. Everyone worked hard for the next few weeks to establish the new town, and it quickly took shape.

It was over two months since the boats had left Waterford for Troy, and they should be well on their way back by now. The new settlers would be tired after their long journey, and their proper welcome to Ériu was important. Cessair knew that it was now time to head back to the east to greet them when they arrived.

At the sea entrance to Broadhaven, there were two great pillars of rock arising out of the sea. There were very distinctive and easily described to new sea captains as the markers for the Broadhaven entrance. These pillars were just offshore from the cliff top where Cessair had seen the great elk standing, so she called the two pillars *'The Stags of Broadhaven.'* On that same clifftop, she ordered a fire to be permanently kept lit as a settlement marker. It would at first serve as a welcome and would also help to guide the arriving settlers, but later still, a lit beacon would help the trading vessels to find their way to Broadhaven.

Ladra wanted to return to Waterford by going down Ériu's West Atlantic coast, but Cessair said that they would take the shorter and smoother route that they had come. Ladra did not argue too much as one of his ships was to be left in Broadhaven, and the other was to be crewed with as few people as possible. Most of the tribe just wanted and were needed to build their new homes and settle quickly in Broadhaven. There were a few like Ladra; they just wanted to travel!

Cessair had also decided that they should call in with Angus, as the newly arriving settlers would need as many axes as they could buy. She was to travel in on an almost empty boat. After a few moments of thinking, she devised a plan that made her feel like a trader. She had her ship filled with goods that she knew were in short supply on Angus' island and that they needed. With the boat loaded and a minimum crew on board, they once more set sail. A few days later, Ladra called out,

"Angus' island is just ahead."

Just as everyone went forward to the bow to get a 'closer' view, Ladra shouted again.

"And he has a visitor!

It looks like a big trading ship."

They arrived at the tiny pier to a big welcome. They had been seen well before Ladra had seen the island; the islanders never missed a business opportunity. But this time, it was not just business. They were welcoming friends. Angus greeted them like long-lost cousins with great hugs and kisses; this surprised Cessair and the rest of her team. Everyone was in great form except for the visiting traders, who were definitely, not happy. They were packing up and very eager to leave quickly.

"Have you room for another passenger?"

They all knew the voice but could not see the person. It was Ladra who answered first.

"If it is OK with Cessair, then you are more than welcome, Antonio."

"Of course it is."

Was the instant shout from Cessair.

"Great, I was hoping to catch up with you all; I have lots of news, and I also want to talk business with you later."

Antonio was in a fluster as he then raced back onto the trading ship to collect his personal items before they departed with them still on board. There was hardly a word spoken with the trading captain as he thanked him for his passage. Antonio left his boat carrying a small bundle under his arm.

Antonio had a broad smile on his face as he re-joined Cessair's party on the pier.

"Phew! That is one angry Sherden captain. He came hoping to buy a large number of axes in exchange for a few clay pots but found instead that Angus had learnt how to make his own! No more dirt-cheap axes here.

*To make the trader's annoyance worse, these are the best axes in the world, and he **has** to buy them; his best customers demand them! He had to pay a small fortune for just a few axes. It serves him right; I say, he charges a large fortune for them!"*

Cessair turned to Angus and said.

"I hope that you have some axes left for us. Come on board, look at what we have, and see if we can trade."

Angus eagerly boarded and looked at what they had brought. He had a great grin on his face as he said.

"Cessair, you are a natural trader! You saw the things that we were short of on this island, and you have saved us a considerable amount of work in gathering them and transporting them here ourselves. We are better spending our time making axes than travelling to the mainland in our tiny boats and looking or foraging for these items.

I will take it all and have my people help unload it and load our axes, arrowheads and spearheads onto your boat."

The deal was done, and everyone was happy.

The night was drawing in, and Angus invited the small travelling party up to his home to stay the night and to catch up with the news of Ériu's growing tribes. Angus never mentioned the pot-making lessons as Antonio was present, but Antonio already had his suspicions.

Life, The Universe and Everything; The Ancients.

Early the following day, at sunrise, Ladra had untied his boat, ready to head south. Most of the village was at the pier to see their friends leave, even after such a short stay. Angus promised to build up a large stock of stonework goods for the new settlers. The deal would last for many years as long as they kept supplying them with mainland supplies.

They were comforted by the great islander's words as they drew away from the pier.

"The spirits have given you a great wind for your journey, and you should reach your destination late today."

The ship set off so fast that Cessair only had time to shout out a brief *"Thank you."*

And with that fleeting acknowledgement, they rapidly returned to Bridget's extra holy site of Sí an Bhrú.

Antonio took the chance to bring his friends up to date with the news around the Mediterranean. After a few minutes of the latest news, he spoke these words of warning.

"Your ships going to Troy stopped in Sardinia for supplies. I knew one of your captains, and we spent a great evening talking about Ériu. He showed me the rock that he was carrying, and I told him to keep it very secret from everyone outside of Troy. It is very valuable, and everyone will want it. You must be very careful who finds out about it, and you must choose carefully those you want to work with. Whomever you may tell, you must make sure that the pirates never learn about it.

I know our Santorini tradesmen would be very keen to trade for it. That is why I took a lift with the trading ship passing close to your land, hoping to meet up with you."

During the different conversations, Antonio asked about Banba and what she was doing. Cessair knew not to probe any further, but his interest in Banba was registered in her mind.

Angus had been right, and just as the darkness started falling, they saw the signal fire at the mouth of the River Bóinne. As they approached closer, they saw a large ship coming from the other direction. The wind was not as strong as when they left Angus, but they still travelled quite quickly with the wind still behind them. The other ship was sailing against the wind, so it was making plodding progress even though it was much closer to the signal fire. Both ships arrived at the mouth of the river at the same time. The wind was still relatively strong, and docking with the other boat would be unsafe. Ladra brought the two ships close enough that he could shout to their captain.

It turned out that as soon as Ladra saw the captain, he recognised him immediately as the first ship back with the next troop of settlers. The other captain was delighted that he now had a guide for the final part of his journey through unknown waters. A flash of light at sea caught Ladra's attention; it was still some distance away. He saw a few more flashes, and then he realised that the rest of the new settlers' ships were signalling with their reflective dishes. They, too, had seen the fire, and they now knew where they were going. It would be almost dark by the time the rest of the fleet would catch up, but Ladra knew that it was safest for him to take the lead ship ahead and send a small boat back to lead the rest to the safety of the river.

Cessair and Bridget were on deck watching while all of this was going on. Bridget had become very tense since the boats met at sea, and she was very quiet for a while, and then she spoke.

"Cailtach was on that ship! That ship is carrying the tribe from Egypt. She is the most senior High Priestess in Egypt – why is she here? She usually never leaves Saqqara!

Cessair was a little surprised that such an important Druid should come to her land so soon. She asked.

"Are you sure? Why would she come here? Did you send for her?"

"I could never just send for her."

Replied Bridget, she was shocked at the thought, and she went on.

"She is so important, and I am sure that she hardly even knows that I exist!

I sent back detailed reports of my earliest findings with the Merkhet, even before we found Sí an Bhrú. I am sure that she would not have even seen them.

I don't know why she is here!"

Cessair's reply was pragmatic.

"We will find out soon enough.

I met her once when Saball took me to Giza to see the work progress there. She met us because she had to; not even she could avoid meeting the Pharaoh and his guests!"

A few minutes later, she continued.

"Look, they have already built a pier, and there, just ahead, are all the small boats waiting to take us all upriver.

Brace yourself, Bridget; she is already disembarking and making her way here. We will have our answers in a few minutes."

Cailtach did not go straight to the leader of Ériu as would generally be expected. Instead, she left the pier altogether and stood on the dry land and immediately took out and consulted her Merkhet.

It was only seconds before she strode over to where Cessair, Fintan, Bith and Bridget stood. She knew who everyone was, but even so, Cailtach's first few words surprised everyone.

"Cessair, I apologise for my rudeness and my unannounced arrival. I am so excited that I can hardly contain myself. I just had to come as quickly as possible. Please indulge me a little longer, and I will explain everything later."

Without even waiting for a reply from Cessair, she continued.

*"You must be Bridget. I read your reports and just knew that if even a part of what you said is correct, then I **have** to be here. I know we are close. Have you found it? Have you found Dagda's home?*

Many years earlier in Troy, meeting Saball again had overwhelmed Bith; he had overlooked procedure in his excitement. Cessair recognised the same excitement in Cailtach and decided that, once again, she should let it pass and let Bridget answer her questions.

On the other hand, Bridget was in much more of a fluster. Standing in front of her was the most important and knowledgeable druid in the world, asking her if she had found the home of the most ancient of gods. She knew the place was important but had not made the connection with Dagda. Thinking about it, she had not even reported this site to anyone yet. How did Cailtach know? She felt that she should just say, what she knew, rather than what she thought.

"I do know that this land of Ériu is special and that I have never before had such responses from my Merkhet. I also know that the strongest messages have come from a hill close to here. We call it Sí an Bhrú."

"Please take me there as quickly as possible."

Asked the Egyptian druid, who had not felt such passion or anticipation for many years. She turned to Cessair pleading.

"May I ask Bridget to take me there right now? This is so important. My research in Saqqara and Giza strongly suggests that the land that you call Ériu is of immense importance, and when I read Bridget's reports, I could hardly believe them. They fit so well with my research; I just had to see for myself. Even at this distance, my Merkhet tells me that this place is very important. I know that it will soon be very dark, but I must see it today – please!

Cessair was again surprised by her almost childish passion and enthusiasm. To be so excited, having just come off a boat after so many days of travelling, just underlined her commitment. Cessair still wanted to assert her authority; after all, Ériu was still 'her' land.

"Please accompany me on this boat with my party. We will go up the river to our new settlement. From there, Bridget will walk you

up the hill to Sí an Bhrú. Everyone has travelled far and is very tired,
and I insist you join my party and me at my home in an hour for a
meal and a good night's rest."

Those were almost the only words Cessair had with Cailtach until much later that night.

Cailtach quizzed Bridget with numerous questions during the whole boat trip. As soon as they landed, she was the first off the boat. She led Bridget up the hill to the seat of the god's power.

There were many new houses built while Cessair was away in Broadhaven, and she was very impressed with all of the work done. They had even built her a fine new home for when she came to visit them. Cessair thought it was a very extravagant gesture, especially as there was so much more building to do and yet she appreciated all the work they had gone to just to honour her. She now had plenty of room for her important guest.

There was great excitement as one boatload after another brought a new tribe to Ériu. They met the residents who had worked so hard to make new homes for their arrival. There was a great buzz in the air, with the new settlers all wanting to learn about Ériu while everyone else wanted to hear about news of their friends left in Troy. The most important topic for discussion was the arrival of such a famous druid as Cailtach. Cessair laughed to herself when she saw all of the resident druids in as much of a fluster as Bridget was and as they scurried up the hill to catch a glimpse of her in person.

Bridget brought Cailtach down to Cessair's new home at the right time, even though their prestigious visitor was still so excited. The formal setting of the shared meal brought Cailtach back into the land of the people.

She felt that she should explain herself to Cessair. This was new to Cailtach. Back in Egypt, Cailtach was answerable to no one other than the Pharaoh, of course. But here, she had great respect for Cessair, what she had achieved, and what she was doing in this extraordinary and holy land.

Life, The Universe, and Everything; The Ancients.

It was respect for Cessair, the person, rather than the importance of her earthly role, that compelled Cailtach to explain her behaviour and the importance of Sí an Bhrú to the world!

"Everything is made of cells of energy at very many different levels and sizes. Even the world around us is made up of its own type of cell. Think of a cell as being everything within a bubble. Like people, each cell bubble seems to be independent and self-sufficient. But to live, all cells, like people, need other cells around them. Communication methods between people use our senses, such as talking to each other, which connects them and enhances them. All cells are connected in many different ways, and when the cells are pieces of space or land, we call the communication lines between them 'Ley Lines.' These Ley Lines are the communication ways that the spirits, we call ancients, made and use.

I know, Cessair, that this all sounds complicated, but when we find these Ley Lines, we can communicate directly with the Ancients."

Cessair asked.

"Bridget showed me how the ancients helped us find the water underground with a Hazel stick. An ancient connected and controlled my hands on that Hazel branch. Are those Ley Lines?"

"Not really. I told you it was complicated. Water also has important communication properties that the Ancients used. But you are certainly on the right idea."

It was a very long time since Cailtach spoke about such things with anyone, not alone to someone who was not a druid. She liked Cessair's inquiring mind, and she also knew that Cessair was someone exceptional.

"I have studied these lines for most of my life and know that finding one as strong as the line at Giza is extraordinary. The line here is much more powerful and is, therefore, much closer to the heart of Dagda's power. Bridget did not exaggerate about what she found, and I, too, have now found a place much closer to Dagda."

Cessair was now fully engaged and eager to learn more about this mighty god that could be sensed just up the hill from where she was sitting.

"Please tell me about Dagda. Why did Tabiti make him?

The depth of Cessair's question impressed Cailtach, so she gave her a detailed reply.

"Tabiti created chaos. It had no shape or purpose, like a pile of fresh clay. She then gave it shapes or forms when she moulded it into everything that could be seen or touched. At this stage, they were just things, ornaments if you like to think of them as such.

Tabiti then breathed fire into some of them. One of these objects was our sun. She then created, from her essence, Ancients that could flow easily between all of these things and could fashion or observe what was going on in her new creation. The ornaments were now different, but they still lacked something essential, and that was a purpose or, put another way, a reason to continue to be there.

She then breathed a piece of her essence into these 'ornaments' because she wanted to experience being a tree, a person, a fish, a river, or even a Hazel stick – we also call these parts of her, Ancients.

The experience was to be the purpose and to be enjoyed by her essence, also called Ancients, in all of her forms. Now she just had one more thing to do, and that was to create time. Time is so important that she created the Ancient called Dagda to manage it.

Dagda creates and controls time. Time allows purpose."

Cessair's next question was.

"What is our purpose? Why are we here?"

Cailtach had already anticipated it, but she was glad that Cessair had asked it because it showed that she was following and understanding her. Cailtach continued seamlessly.

"Time gives meaning to 'our' birth; when 'our' soul, that is to say, our Ancient, that original piece of Tabiti, we sometimes wrongly call 'I,' starts to experience our unique cell as life. Most people believe that they are alone and that the rest of the universe is outside of them – something else, something independent of them, everything that is not 'I' – their cell remains limited, small, and isolated.

We, as druids, know that we are intimately part of the essence of Tabiti but that we can only usually relate to the cell created around us, and we call that small cell 'I'. We strive to connect to as many different cells around us to allow us to see more glimpses of Tabiti.

Just as it is essential to have something start, it is also necessary for the purpose to have an end or a goal – we, in our little cells called 'I', wrongly call this end death.

When Dagda removes time for a cell, someone or something dies and merges back into Tabiti. Tabiti now has something else, and it's new and something that she did not have before. She has added the experience and enjoyment of the life lived by each tiny part of her essence.

When we die, our cell widens and now encompasses our experiences and all of the other souls' experiences that different pieces of Tabiti have had. Think of a person's life as a single drop of water, and then that drop falls and returns to the vast ocean. That individual drop dies. It ceases to be a separate unique drop of water but has now become part of something much greater than all of the unique original drops within it.

Cessair, I realise that this is all very complex, but for us, experiencing being people, the most critical resource is time. Dagda controls time, birth, life and death; that is why he is so important to us as people and why we need to learn to understand his messages.

Crops are planted, they grow, they are harvested, and then they die. Dagda manages that process by supplying the time within which everything, even our very lives, happens."

Cessair was mentally exhausted following Cailtach's theory of everything, but she was honoured to be gifted such a lesson in divine knowledge. She unconsciously reached for the tooth around her neck. She missed her friend Dana to help her better understand.

Before finally retiring for the night, Cessair asked if Cailtach had any news of Scotia or of Saball, Scotia's grandfather and Pharoah.

"Scotia has visited Giza many times. She is always there when the Pharaoh visits. She is always particularly interested in going there; she is drawn to the place. She is the Pharaoh's

granddaughter, you see; a lovely, intelligent young woman. Did you meet her when you were living in Meroe?"

Cessair smiled broadly when she realised that Scotia was still visiting Nel. She knew exactly what drew Scotia to Giza, but she would not betray their secret. So instead, Cessair simply replied.

"Yes, I did. She is a lovely young woman."

Cessair showed Cailtach where she should sleep. Once Cailtach saw her comfortable and stationary bed, which did not move with the waves, she found that tiredness quickly overtook her.

Even though Cessair was also very tired, her mind was racing at the implications of finding Dagda's 'home' in Ériu. Fintan's regular but thankfully quiet snoring brought Dagda's time into sharp focus; that is, until she also fell asleep and, for her at least, time was temporally suspended.

Cessair and Fintan were up at dawn and ready to properly see all of the works and progress that had occurred while they had been away. To their surprise, Cailtach had left some time earlier. She had gone with Bridget and all of the other druids to celebrate her first dawn in Ériu at Sí an Bhrú.

Ladra and Antonio joined Cessair for breakfast as they had a lot to discuss. Nine ships were waiting to return to Troy to pick up more settlers. People in Troy were tired of putting their lives on hold, waiting for their passage to Ériu. The captains knew that, at most, they could only make four trips a year and then only if they had no long spells of bad weather.

Plans were made for the return to Troy to meet the next settlers, and the discussion changed to trading when Cailtach and Bridget joined them. Cessair knew that the 'pushy' druid Cailtach was bound to want something new, and she was right. Cailtach's first words were.

"I need my best craftsmen here as soon as possible! This place is unique, and we must build a magnificent monument for Dagda as soon as possible.

I came just to see if Bridget's findings were accurate and then to return to Egypt quickly, but this find here, in Sí an Bhrú, is so important I cannot leave now.

Someone must go to Egypt and bring back my best astrologers. We cannot take them all, as Pharaoh's work must go on, but I must have my best astrologers and master craftsmen build a structure that will allow us to 'see' Dagda's plan for our future and to be able to show that we can understand that plan."

Cessair was quick to reply.

"I cannot send a ship to Egypt now; there are so many people wanting to travel from Troy, it would not be fair to take their places on the ship."

Cailtach suggested.

"The Pharaoh pays us well so we could pay for our passage."

She had no sooner uttered those words than she realised that money was not the issue but rather the lack of boats. It was then that Antonio saw an excellent trading opportunity, and he suggested.

"If I went with your ships and envoy and they stopped in Santorini, I could hire a boat from my friends there to go on to Egypt. I would then bring your astrologers back here. If you had a shipload of that rock of yours, Fintan, I could then take it back to Santorini and sell it; it would more than then pay for the whole trip.

It would mean that no one would lose their passage here from Troy, and you and the people of Santorini would start a trading arrangement that would be profitable to all of us."

Everyone thought that was a great solution, but there was only one problem. Who was going to be the envoy? It had to be someone with authority, a good organiser and also capable of handling people firmly, but also with diplomacy.

Cessair knew exactly the person to send, and she had already promised her such a trip.

Cailtach was reluctant to leave Sí an Bhrú to travel to Waterford. She would not spend her valuable time going to Egypt. Still, she finally accepted that the envoy would need to be appropriately and accurately briefed and that she would need to do that herself directly. She agreed after being told that a boat would quickly bring her back as soon as the briefing was over.

Bridget pointed out the calendar hilltop to Cailtach as the fleet of ships entered the River Suir on their way back to Waterford. She was pleased to have the chance to impress the High Priestess with all of the astrological work that she had carried out over the last year.

Cessair decided to resupply the ships in Waterford for the journey ahead. Ladra also wanted to inspect the vessels while they were stranded on dry sand. The large sandy beaches there were perfect for his purpose.

Banba greeted them at Dún na m-Barc. The ships had been seen as they passed the signal fire on the coast, and word had quickly travelled back to her. She was pleased to see her friends return, surprised to see the High Priestess, and she just stared at Antonio with a stupid grin on her face.

She had not been idle in the months that Cessair had been away, and she had prepared well for the arrival of new settlers. She had also organised provisions for the resupply of their ships.

There was a sense of urgency, and everyone immediately set about his or her task. Fintan took Antonio to see where they collected and prepared the important rock. Bridget showed Cailtach the important Calendar Hill and introduced her to the rest of her local druids, who were all suitably 'star struck.' Ladra beached the ships and inspected their bottoms, and Bith went to see how his precious seeds were growing. Cessair and Banba went to Waterford to look around and talk.

It was sometime later, after the tour, and they were resting with a fine meal in front of them, that Cessair said.

"You know Banba, how I always promised you a trip to Egypt."

Banba had expected to hear many things but not this. She established Waterford, and she was proud of all of her work and her achievements. She had a system, and the town was developing well under her authority. She wanted to stay put when there was still so much to do and organise.

Cessair explained about Cailtach and her need for her to have her best druids brought from Saqqara and Giza to help her in Sí an Bhrú. She explained the importance and authority of the envoy's role and how important this was to the development of Ériu.

"Banba, I also need you to go and see how Scotia is and to bring her all of our news. I miss her, and I worry about her and Nel. Bring Scotia and Saball my little gifts and also tell them our story and about our life here.

You should not be away for too long as Antonio will be your captain. He will hire a new boat in Santorini to take you directly to Egypt and then straight back here."

The news that Antonio was to be her captain for the journey that completely changed Banba's attitude toward the trip, and now she was positively looking forward to it.

Cessair picked up on Banba's rapid change of attitude at the mention of Antonio. She was pleased that her stalwart companion and friend reciprocated Antonio's feelings.

She could not resist a gentle nudge in Banba's back accompanied by some friendly teasing comments.

A few days later, the fleet sailed back down the River Suir and then headed south to the Mediterranean.

The ship with Banba and Antonio on board carried a full load of Fintan's rock. His tribe had been gathering and preparing it for some months and planned to turn it into metal when Fintan returned. So much of it was collected that Fintan could send a shipload off with Antonio. He felt sure that he could easily and quickly gather more when he was ready to smelt it and turn it into copper. Antonio could now sell the load of rock and pay for the hire of a boat in Santorini before he went to Egypt.

Much to his annoyance, Ladra did not go with the fleet. He was needed in Ériu to help with the arrival of all the new settlers and with the communication between the settlements. His town in Wexford needed him, and he was also required to design, build and repair Ériu's boats and ships. Top of his list of eager passengers was Cailtach, who was keen to return to Sí an Bhrú as soon as possible.

Just as Antonio and the fleet reached the open sea and were turning to head south, the next group of ships from Troy met them. The newcomers were in a bad state. Some of their ships looked damaged, with their sails torn. It was fortunate that Banba was on board because she could tell them to change their course and head directly to Waterford, which was only an hour or two away.

There the fleet could make any necessary repairs; give the passengers a needed break and a rest after what was an arduous journey. Once rested and repaired, they could then make the final leg around Ériu to Broadhaven – Cessair would surely agree with her. The sea captains, who were also exhausted, were delighted with the change of plans.

The scouts in Waterford had barely lost sight of the departing ships over the horizon when they saw the next fleet coming towards them. At first, they thought Banba's group had a problem large enough for the whole fleet to return. It was not long before they realised that the Broadhaven-destined ships had changed their plans. The lookout scouts hurried back to Waterford to tell Cessair.

Cessair realised that they must be in difficulty changing their course and plans so radically. So, she immediately instructed Banba to prepare for up to five hundred tired and distressed new settlers.

More Settlers and Ériu Grows.

Ladra immediately took his ship out to sea to greet the bedraggled newcomers and to guide them into port. As he approached them, he saw what a poor shape the boats were in and their torn sails offering poor manoeuvrability. Some were lashed together because they had lost almost all of their sails and needed the support of the other ships so that they could sail at all.

He recognised the exhaustion on the faces of all on board, and so he even had a number of his own crew aboard the stricken ships to help bring them into port. One ship was in such bad shape that he took it directly to ground it on the nearby beach because he knew it would not make it up the River Suir.

Ten boats had made it from Troy, but only nine docked at Dûn na m-Barc. Ladra sent a small fleet of little boats out to collect the passengers that were stranded on the beach.

Every one of those travellers was in an exhausted and pitiful state. They were now so glad to be safe on dry land. Mothers barely had the strength to carry their young children, and most people just left their few personal possessions on board. As they disembarked, the people of Waterford took them away individually or in small groups for food, comfort, and rest.

Once everyone was safely settled and the ships properly docked, Cessair visited Ladra at his house. He had three of the travellers' captains with him, and they were all eating at Ladra's table. Ladra called out.

"Cessair, Fintan, please join us. There is plenty of room.

These captains were just about to tell me what went wrong."

The three newcomers were starting to recover from their extended ordeal and were only now beginning to relax. Just by looking at these men, Cessair could only imagine what they had gone through. The first captain started.

"We were travelling just a few hours behind Cailtach's ships when the winds came from the north. We were too far out to sea and away from the land to seek shelter, and so we decided to try and ride out the strong winds. The winds blew for days; sometimes, it was so strong that the sea had monstrous waves. We knew that we were being blown back south even without our sails up. When they finally did die down, we were lost.

Then we saw land to the south, and we knew that we had seen that coastline before, many days earlier. We had been blown southwards for hundreds of miles. So once more, we retraced our route back north. Then almost two weeks later than expected, we reached Banba's ship just an hour or so from Waterford. She gave us fresh water and told us to come straight here. Thank Tabiti for guiding her to us. Many of our passengers are so weak that they would not have survived the extra week's travel up to our original destination."

Cessair looked at the other captains and realised that they were almost asleep. Ladra quickly guided them all to their beds before returning to the table. He had a worried look on his face as he spoke.

"They were so lucky not to be blown out and lost in that endless Atlantic. If they had not met with Banba, they would have tried to head up to Broadhaven; we would have definitely lost ships and people."

Cessair resolved there and then that she would return to her original plan and bring all new ships arriving in Ériu to Waterford. Then once rested, their passengers and crew would continue and travel on to their final settlement place.

More Settlers and Ériu Grows.

It took many days for the weakened travellers to recover from their ordeal, and many did not want to board any ship, not alone the one on which they had such a horrific experience. Their good experience of Ériu in Waterford meant that they just wanted to stay and settle there.

Cessair told them about Broadhaven, the land in the sea she named after the fish and about the excellent area for farming that was already being prepared for them. She told them about the great trading opportunity with the purple dye and other local resources. She told them that their route to Broadhaven would always be close to the coast and that there were many safe places to shelter if the wind blew too strongly. Finally, it was the promise that she and Ladra would go with them to show them the way that finally persuaded them to go.

Bith and Fintan would not travel with them this time as they both had their own important missions. The next tribes would all need their areas to settle in, but they would also need support and help to establish their new homes. The places had to be far enough from the established towns so as not to crowd that town's expansion but still close enough for the existing tribes to be able to help them.

Bith wanted to find several new sites, for he knew that in the next couple of years, there would be at least fifty tribes or new communities in Ériu. Several sites had been found in Broadhaven and a few around Sí an Bhrú, but as all of the new settlers were landing in Waterford, this area needed the most sites.

Fintan saw the power of commerce. He also saw how valuable the rock in Ériu could be, but he also knew that if he smelted the rock himself here in Ériu, the metal would be much more valuable. The people with all of the right skills were already in his town. He had smelted the rock in Affreidg, and he and his specialists were masters in their field. It was great that Antonio thought that the stone was so valuable that he should take it back to Santorini, but the real value was to be made by making and selling the metal. He had already found a rich deposit of great rock and had asked his FirGaileoin to go and dig this rock free and for the Firbolg to gather it up in their bags and carry it to the nearby wood where they would prepare it and then smelt it. One shipload of the finished metal was worth dozens of boats full of the rock. If they could find gold, then they would have an even more valuable product to sell.

Cessair, Bridget and Cailtach were once again on Ladra's boat as he led the small fleet away from Waterford and headed up the coast. The expedition was to spend the night in the shelter of the river mouth close to Sí an Bhrú, and they would be ready for the dawn start the following day. Ladra took his boat up to the pier and tied it up his boat. There a welcoming committee were delighted to see Cailtach return. Everyone was keen to start and build the monument to Dagda, but no one was confident enough to start anything without her. They had, however, built her a fine new roundhouse. Cailtach transferred into a small boat ready for the short trip up the river to the settlement at Sí an Bhrú. As she was about to leave, she spoke to Cessair.

"This place is so special, Ériu is so special, and you, too, Cessair, are so special. You were all destined for each other; this was and is your 'Land of Destiny.'

With those enigmatic, almost mystical words, she was gone.

A few days later, Ladra spied the fire by the Stags and shortly afterwards, the fleet disgorged hundreds of excited new settlers. Even in the few weeks that they had been away, the works at Broadhaven had progressed well. There was even a pier already constructed, and a second one was half-built. Some roundhouses could shelter many of the new arrivals, and Cessair was impressed that they had already created their own Broadhaven community identity.

The ships' captains had all been well-rested in Waterford, and they were all keen to head back to Troy as quickly as possible. They

More Settlers and Ériu Grows.

took on board fresh food, water, and a few trading items to see if they would sell well back in Troy. They also took with them a number of the Brehons and Bards, whose tribes were waiting to come to Ériu. It was their job to tell the new tribes about Ériu and its laws; Cessair wanted them to be fully informed about where they were going and, most importantly, the rules of their new country.

Cessair was not going to stay either, as she was keen to explore the river that led to the inland freshwater sea that Angus had told her about. She also wanted to be in Waterford in time for the next shiploads of settlers. Ladra said that they should leave immediately and travel with all of the rest of the captains, at least until they reached the mouth of the river that they wanted to follow. And so, after only three days at Broadhaven, Cessair, Bridget, and Ladra were once again at sea. This time however they towed behind them two much smaller boats to explore the river and the inland sea that it led to.

It was easy to find the mouth of the river that they wanted; Angus's instruction was simple to follow, he had said.

"It is easy to find. Ten miles of pure flat sand mark the mouth of two rivers. The river that joined at the west end had a large estuary but a small river, while at the other end of the strand was a large river with no widened estuary. It was this larger river that led to the inland sea."

The river was large, but nothing like as big as the river in Egypt. Even so, Ladra managed to navigate a short way up against the flow because he had a strong wind behind him. But the time came when he stopped the ship and said that the rest of the journey upriver would need to be on the much smaller boats.

A few people were left on board the ship while everyone else boarded the two boats. They knew that they would be away for several days and so they brought with them supplies, weapons and shelter.

They had not been travelling for long, and they were making good progress upriver when they heard the wolves. They knew that cry all too well, and they immediately looked for their weapons. They were perfectly safe, as the river was very wide, and they knew the wolves would not threaten them there.

Cessair said.

"They are hunting something. That is a pack ready to make a kill. At least they will eat well tonight!"

"Look!"

Ladra shouted. He was pointing to the riverbank, not very far away. There, they saw a middle-aged man and a youth surrounded by the pack. They had tried to head for the safety of the water, but the wolves had cut them off and encircled them. The man and the brave youth were back-to-back, trying to keep off the wolves, but each time they faced a wolf in front of them, another would start an attack from the side. If there had been only one man, he would have been eaten by now, but the duo could keep the wolves at bay, for a while at least. They were noticeably very tired, and the wolves sensed their weakness. They were now ready for a full-pack attack to finish them off.

Immediately both of the boats were turned and were headed straight to the riverbank to help the two men in trouble. The wolves were not to be deterred from the meal that they had worked so hard for, and they stood their ground. If anything, the arrival of extra people would hasten their final attack. The pack's leader was a huge animal, and it was clearly focused on its quarry directly in front and was now only one leap away from dinner.

The alpha male wolf had little experience with men. Several noisy two-legged creatures on the water's edge, still many meters away, were not seen as a threat to him. With his narrow-set eyes evolved to see prey directly in front of him accurately, he probably never even saw the hail of arrows coming at him from his side. Many hit their target, and the alpha male hunter had itself been hunted and killed.

With their leader dead, the rest of the pack fell into complete disarray, and they quickly ran off into the surrounding woods. The two strangers fell to the ground in exhaustion and relief – they were so lucky to be still alive.

The two men were wearied and just continued to sit on the ground. Cessair reached them first, and she offered them water to drink; it was served with a friendly smile. She asked if they were ok, but it was soon evident that they did not understand her words at all. While they did not understand her words, they did understand their meaning; her sympathy and help spoke with language beyond words.

The two slowly rose to their feet and started to talk in their own language. Cessair did not understand what they said, but Ladra recognised a few words. He said something, only three small words, but that was enough, and the older man instantly smiled, laughed, and embraced him. Ladra then said to Cessair.

"I recognise some of this language. It is spoken by those who live in the country north of the Pillars of Hercules. I do not understand it, but some of my sea friends taught me this phrase."

Cessair did not ask what he had just said to them as she already had a good idea of what sailors had learned to say in every language. The important message is that he had created a shared link between the two strangers and his tribe.

The man pointed to himself and said.

"Capa."

He pointed to the youth and said.

"Laigne."

He then looked at Cessair with an expression that he was awaiting a reply. She then pointed at each person around her and called out their names. The last of her companions to be named was Ladra, and as soon as she had spoken his name, the stranger's face brightened up, and he pointed at Cessair and said in a bold voice.

"Ceeessa!"

94

She did not even try to correct him! He knew her name. Here in the remotest part of the world that she knew – he knew her name!

He showed Cessair his boat, which was only a few metres from where he had been attacked but could not reach it while the wolves surrounded them. He and Laigne boarded it and beckoned Cessair and her people to follow him. They followed Capa's boat until he headed to the bank at the bottom of a small but steep slope.

Cessair saw a wooden palisade at the top of the hill. This was a small settlement, and other people were living there along with Capa. A small group of about ten men came to the water's edge when they saw the strangers following their man. Many carried weapons, but no one was threatening. Ladra gently touched Cessair's side and pointed a little upstream at the riverbank. There, there was a ship moored, looking as though it was ready to go at short notice.

Capa and his young companion spoke quickly and excitedly to his tribe; he then waved to Cessair and the other boat members to join them on land. As Cessair and her crew climbed the hill to the palisade, many happy people surrounded them, and she was well accepted and made to feel very comfortable and at ease. Once inside the barrier, another older man joined Capa. He spoke in a language that Cessair did understand.

"My name is Luasad. Our people know of you, and we welcome you. Angus, who lives on an island in the sea not far from here, has told us about you. He said that you might visit. We welcome you as our first visitors. Until now, the terrible wolves were the only creatures to show interest in us. To protect ourselves, we built this palisade."

People surrounded the fire, bringing fruits, nuts and all sorts of meat and fish. They had never before had visitors, and Cessair was their first, so they were going to make it an occasion to remember. Furthermore, in their eyes, she was the most famous person in the world!

Cessair learnt that Capa, a doctor, and Luasad were the leaders of a group who travelled from Iberia each year to gather the eels and other produce from this island. When winter approached, they would sail back south to their homes and families in Iberia. They only lived here for the summer, and they sent their finds and kills back to Iberia in a ship that constantly travelled up and down.

"So, you do not live here all year. Do you farm and grow food?

Asked Cessair. As she spoke, she looked around, but she saw no crops or even any domesticated animals. Luasad explained that they did not farm at all and just lived off the land. They found that the river and the great lake some way up had many huge eels and that they were valuable back in their home country. He had found that the best place to catch the eels was at one of the small rapids just further up the River Li. Capa was a doctor searching for new medicines; there were many to be found in this land.

Cessair explained that they were looking for new places to settle new arrivals and that they were on their way up the river to find the big freshwater sea. She also assured Capa and Luasad that they would not take their hunting lands or their fishing areas.

Luasad then said.

"We will show you the way to the great freshwater lake. We are going to fish where the river flows out of the lake; that is where we catch the best eels. It is, though, a lot further than we normally travel."

The next day three boats travelled up the River Li.

It was hard work rowing the boat up the river where there was a swift current. Frequently for these difficult stretches of fast water, they found it easiest to walk along the riverbank while pulling the boats with long hemp ropes or even carrying them overland.

It took most of a full day to reach the great lake, and everyone was pleased to camp on its shore just next to where the Li flowed from it. Cessair smelt the air; she tasted the water. She listened to the sounds of the lake, and in her thoughts, she was once more back by the lakes of old Affreidg.

Travel was much easier and faster on the great lake, so in a few days, they sailed around it. They found many places for new settlements, and several rivers were entering it that just had to be explored at a later date. Cessair thought.

"This area will be great for those tribes who miss Affreidg and who do not like the sea."

She thought about her father, who was never really happy with the unpredictability of the sea and how this freshwater would not harm his crops. She then thought about Capa and Luasad before speaking to Bridget about them.

"They are kind people, but they just come to Ériu and take. They seem to respect little, and they certainly do not put anything back! They do not even want to live here! How can they not see the beauty of this place? How can they not feel the Ancients all around? They are missing out on so much."

Bridget's straightforward reply surprised Cessair, but she knew it to be true.

"It is their greed and worship of financial wealth that hides the Ancients from them."

The journey back down the Li turned out to be much quicker. The current was with them. They stopped briefly at Capa's camp before re-joining their ship and headed once more out to sea.

Several days later, they were safely back in Waterford in good time to meet the next batch of settlers from Troy. Cessair was pleased to be reunited with Fintan and they were all able to be able to relax for a few days.

Everything was starting to fall into place. Fintan had started to smelt copper and had found rich deposits of the valuable ore. Gold and silver had also been found in the rivers. Now all they had to do was see where these precious metal ores had come from. They cleared trees used to smelt the copper and also created create more space to grow more and more crops.

The food plants that Bith had brought as seeds grew well in Ériu. Even if they did not grow as fast, their yields were larger, and they still multiplied quickly. These seeds were being distributed to the other settlements in Ériu and growing well there. Their reliance on hunting and scavenging was reducing as their farming practices produced more and more edible foods.

They collected and separated large quantities of the purple dyes and found several other valuable commodities that they could sell to the rest of their world.

Even the spirits seemed to be happy that they were here in this land of plenty.

Cessair watched as another batch of settlers arriving from Troy docked at the Dûn na m-Barc. She already had their new home area prepared, and after a short break in Waterford, they would soon move on to their final destination.

Then, she recognised the captain of the unknown ship that had just docked; it was Antonio. She was just about to call out to him when the excited but familiar voice of Banba said.

More Settlers and Ériu Grows.

"I have so much exciting news to tell you!"

Fini Volume 3.

Postscript Volume Three.

The exact landing point of Cessair in Ireland has been debated widely using ancient documents that are extant. The location of Waterford fulfilled not only the constraints dictated by the 'Book of the Taking of Ireland' but also fit well for numerous practical purposes. The boats leaving the Mediterranean and 'hugging' the continental coastline would have been swept up first by the Iberian Poleward Current that seamlessly morphs into the European Slope Current. They would have been brought directly into the Irish sea. Waterford lies closest to the UK mainland in the south Irish sea and, therefore, would have been perceived as the nearest destination for sea travellers seeking Ireland.

No one knows when the Brehon system was started but its fundamental tenement of respect not only for people but also for 'nature' in most, if not all senses, hints at a society that lived along with rather than just off the land. This sense of sharing with nature, fundamental to sustainable farming, seems to have been well established by the earliest Scythian societies that developed farming practices many millennia before the Black Sea flood.

This southeastern corner of Ireland became famous for its copper and gold deposits – more about this in later volumes.

Many works have been written about the antiquities of the Boyne Valley and the siting of the major Irish ley line that passes between Newgrange and Tara, then leads across Ireland through Loughcrew, Carrowkeel, Carrowmore and Knocknarea.

Extending a straight line southeastward from Knocknarea, it passes through Stonehenge and other important religious sites in Europe before it reaches Giza. Many volumes testify to the Egyptian connection and also to the technical competence of the Irish Druids, who started building Newgrange before the pyramids were built at Giza. Pendulum finds are copious in most Neolithic Druidic sites, but they are usually recorded as neck pendants. Again, many volumes are written about the use of pendulums and water dowsing. Some people argue that the spirals of early Irish art on ancient sites are the graphic reproduction of paths of pendulums under different influences. I find it astounding that the above-mentioned important ley line in Ireland closely follows the 'joining' line of two widely separated continents that merged 350 million years ago to bring Northern Ireland and Scotland on one continent into contact with southern Ireland and England on another – a shadow of a more profound mysticism felt by those better in tune with Gaia?

In their thousands, Porcellanite rocks found only on Rathlin Island and one other site, a mountain site on the north Irish coast, have been found fashioned into axes and arrowheads. Some were found many hundreds and, in some cases, thousands of miles away from their origin. These Neolithic artefacts had travelled as far as the Eastern Mediterranean; 5000 years ago, at least some, and probably most, of their journey was by sea.

DNA evidence of a Neolithic burial site on Rathlin Island showed that the interred woman was descended from an early farming tribe living in the area of the Black Sea. DNA of the Neolithic UK tribes inferred that they were descended from hunter-gathers from northern Europe.

One of the earliest inhabited sites found in Ireland was in Mount Sandal on the River Bann (Li in ancient manuscripts), which was recorded as one of the original rivers of Ireland by the old chroniclers. Excavations suggest that this site was occupied by transient hunter-gathers as there was no evidence of farming. The ancient Irish texts refer to people in the exact location as the earliest people to visit Ireland, but they only seasonally used the place as a source of 'exotic' goods.

Some sources even claim that the naming of the 'Britons' (the islands England and Ireland) came from the Scythian-derived sea traders who called them the "Fire (Bri) Islands (tons)." Named as such because the trading ships that gathered raw materials and supplies from them used permanently lit fires for navigation purposes.

Series Synopsis.

This series of books have been written to offer an alternative history of Ireland. A story about the little island in the Atlantic Ocean that has influenced and benefitted the whole known world.

These books are written, for a broad audience, in a readable story format. They introduce Cessair, the original settler who worked with nature, Partholon an exploiting businessman, Phoenician sea traders, Fomorian sea pirates, The FirBolg or Bag Men, The Tuathe de Danan, who were the Druids or magic people and the Milesians, the descendants of Scotia the daughter of an Egyptian Pharoah, plus many others.

These books have been written to inspire an interest in investigating what really happened to the peoples on the island of Ireland since the Ice Age. The author has drawn evidence from ancient texts and associated commentaries. He has added the latest scientific findings and analysis to construct a possible and plausible history that is free of political bias.

Successive conquering invaders have written Ireland's popular history. It has been written to glorify and justify why the island was invaded rather than face many uncomfortable truths. Truths such as the enforced annulment of equal status and power of women. Equality and respect had been enshrined in Irish Brehon law from the earliest of times.

The series starts with the flooding of a vast area of highly fertile land 7600 years ago; this area is now known as 'The Black Sea.' It follows the stories of characters named in the ancient Irish texts that changed Ireland. It describes how the farming and metalworking Irish stood well apart from the rest of the hunter-gatherers in Northern Europe and how, instead, they had close ties with the Eastern Mediterranean and Egypt via the then very active sea routes.

The series covers the collapse of the Mediterranean civilisation at the end of the Bronze Age. Later volumes show how Ireland led the Isles of Britain to be the first area in the world to declare itself Christian in AD 250, well before Rome and centuries before St Patrick arrived!

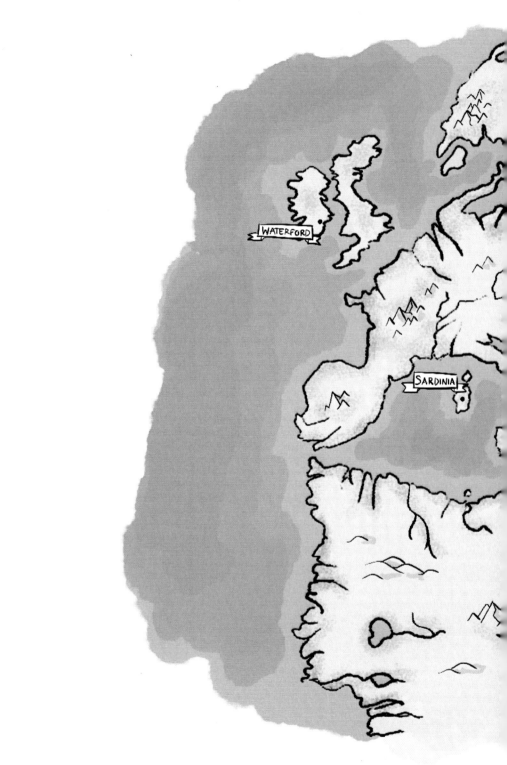